Face Everything and Rise

Letting Go: A Story of Change and Transformation

DanThy Nguyen

BALBOA.PRESS
A DIVISION OF HAY HOUSE

Balboa Press books may be ordered through booksellers or by contacting:

Balboa Press
A Division of Hay House
1663 Liberty Drive
Bloomington, IN 47403
www.balboapress.com.au
AU TFN: 1 800 844 925 (Toll Free inside Australia)
AU Local: (02) 8310 7086 (+61 2 8310 7086 from outside Australia)

Print information available on the last page.

ISBN: 978-1-5043-2216-4 (sc)
ISBN: 978-1-5043-2217-1 (e)

Balboa Press rev. date: 01/05/2022

An Invitation

* *

Dear Reader,
You are invited to:
Face Everything and Rise (the acronym of this is FEAR)

Venue:
I had been procrastinating for a month and a half because of precisely this. How was I going to write about this very topic if I couldn't *Face Everything and Rise* and start writing my book? This book explores stories I have observed that illustrate this, as well as exploring my own journey of change and transformation—a journey I feel is still playing out.

Date and Time:
Are you ready to join me on this journey? Thank you for joining me. Strap in and enjoy the ride. This is a continuous journey which may not have an end date at the end of this book. Along this journey, I hope to provide insights, anecdotes, and strategies that I have found can be applied to *Face Everything and Rise*. These strategies are applied at different stages of the journey which we will explore together. It may not mean that we let go of fear completely; this journey is also about being brave. As Neil Gaiman states in his book *Coraline*, "Being brave doesn't mean you aren't scared. Being brave means you are scared, really scared, badly scared, and you do the right thing anyway."

RSVP*

By opening this book and reading, you have automatically provided your response. Sit back and enjoy!

*When I was younger, I was curious about what RSVP stood for. I learned French in high school and discovered the meaning. RSVP is an initialism derived from the French phrase *Répondez s'il vous plaît*, meaning "Please respond" to require confirmation of an invitation. If this is the main takeaway you get from this book, then at least you have learned something new!

Dedication

I dedicate this book to everyone who encouraged me, supported me, and helped me face my FEAR to *Forget Everything and Rise.* Many people have helped me in various ways. Although I cannot mention them all here, I'd like to mention a few.

My late grandma, who passed away in September 2018.

My mum, who has faced many challenges in her life and is still rising.

My daughter, who is my little firecracker, who, despite her birth complications, is both resilient and compassionate.

My husband, whom I love dearly. Even though we have our differences, he has always been there for me.

My dearest friend, Jeff Lim, whom I have known for over forty years and whom I describe as like a brother to me.

A handful of friends, who have been there for me in my darkest times: Nicole Arslan, Kevin Flynn, Steve Miller, Bill Gooch, Aida Almeida, and Dorothy Olter. I am also thankful for Dax Knight, whom I have coached and who has also coached me in the last twelve months.

I thank everyone for their various means of support, even if it wasn't directly for this book; they have all contributed to my change and transformation in some way. Their support and encouragement are much appreciated. As my friend Bill mentioned to me in conversation, "Friends are the family you choose." Isn't this a lovely way to view your friends—as people you have chosen as your family!

"Being genetically related doesn't make you family. Love, support, trust, sacrifice, honesty, protection, acceptance, security, compromise, gratitude, respect and loyalty are what make you family."

Educate. Inspire. Change.

Début

. . . .

*M*y journey of change started about twenty-two years ago. The catalyst was a near-fatal car accident. I was in intensive care for six weeks, and there was a little hope of survival. Thankfully, I did survive, but not unscathed. I do not remember the accident because of head injuries I sustained, and because of this, I was in an induced coma. I also sustained other injuries. As I was in an induced coma, the nursing staff could not check if I had been paralysed due to my head injuries; if so, they would not have been able to analyse the extent of the paralysis or if my mental capacity had been affected. It was a waiting game.

I have been advised of the full extent of my injuries:

- fluid in the brain
- a C2 fracture in my spine
- fluid in my lungs
- compartment syndrome in my right arm
- compound fracture in my right elbow

Due to the compartment syndrome in my right arm, it swelled up to about three times its normal size. The emergency staff at Alice Springs Hospital were worried about the swelling and feared circulation problems. As a result, my right arm was cut open from the wrist to the elbow to reduce the swelling by relieving pressure. While this may have saved my life, it introduced a new problem: because my arm was three times its normal size, the doctors could not close the cut. As a result, skin grafts were taken from the top of my thighs to graft the cut closed. I have a large skin graft on my right arm, which has left extensive scarring. Most people assume I have been badly burnt until they ask me.

Because of my memory loss, I have relied on others to tell me the cause of the accident. I was the driver at the time and swerved to avoid a goanna sunning on the road on the Stuart Highway, Northern Territory, while returning from Uluru. I was told it was a large goanna—about half the size of the lane! I was driving back to Alice Springs to return the car before boarding a flight home. However, I never made the flight, and neither did my passenger. I do not remember the accident, and I do not remember driving, but I do remember having breakfast with my colleague before walking to the car, and I do remember walking to the driver's side. That is all I can recollect of that day. The events of that day and the following five to six weeks are mainly a recollection of various stories told to me by my family and passenger that day, who sustained less serious injuries. Damn that goanna! Another work colleague said I should have run over it, but I said my first instinct is not to hurt an animal. I never realised this would one day be to my detriment.

My first recollection of the whole experience after the accident was about six weeks afterwards. I recollect a phone call I received from my mother's friend's son. We had been friends for a few years while I was studying at university, but have drifted apart after we finished university and having our own families. He had called to check on me, and I remember telling him I was being transferred to Sydney. I was currently in Royal Adelaide Hospital, having been transferred from Alice Springs Hospital, as the facilities and care I would receive in Adelaide were better than what Alice Springs had to offer. As my condition stabilised, I was now being transferred to the Prince of Wales Hospital in Sydney. I was no longer in an induced coma, was off life support, was more aware, and would be closer to my family.

My mother said I had been on life support for about three weeks and that the nurses would check with her to see if she wanted me to remain on life support or was willing to let me go. Apparently, there had been unsuccessful attempts to take me off life support, so, as per protocol, the nurses checked with the family (my mum) for their wishes. I am fortunate that my mum wished to keep me on life support. She had hope when most people did not. My mum flew to Adelaide and stayed in the hospital residence, visiting me every day. I was unaware of her presence and of my family's visit while I was at the Royal Adelaide Hospital. In total, I was in the Royal Adelaide Hospital for about six weeks. My mum said the care I received from the nurses was exceptional. I owe my life to them. However, I was advised there was one nurse who doubted my survival. Even if she felt that way, she probably shouldn't have expressed it aloud. When I was able to return to work, one of my colleagues, who had called the hospital to ask if she could send flowers to the Intensive Care ward, told me that the nurse who had answered the phone said it might be better to send a wreath! I find humour in that now; however, in hindsight, I feel it was an insensitive thing to say about someone in intensive care.

My memories of my hospital stay relate mostly to my transfer to the Prince of Wales Hospital in Sydney. I was looked after by a team of nurses, a neurosurgeon, and orthopaedic surgeon. I don't remember everyone's names, but I do remember the orthopaedic surgeon's name: Professor Sonobend. He performed surgery on my right arm to place it in a more functional position, as it had become locked at the elbow due to extra bone growth around the compound fracture. I was informed that extra bone growth happened due to my head injury. If not for this surgery, I wouldn't be able to work, write, type, drive, or do many of the things I have been able to do. For this, I am eternally grateful for his foresight.

My recovery from the accident was a long and arduous process. I was not able to work for almost a year. A lot of physical and emotional healing took place during this time. Think about how you would feel, a twenty-three-year-old who is relatively fit and healthy, and suddenly your health and independence are stripped away. At some stages of my recovery, I wasn't feeling too great. At times, I did feel sorry for myself. I remember being at home one day. I was slowly getting some of my independence back but frustrated at my inability to put my hair up into a ponytail due to my fixed elbow. It was only a small thing, but when you think about it, it's usually the small things that set you off, isn't it? So, I was feeling sorry for myself and needed to tie my hair up into a ponytail. It bothered me because I couldn't do it and had to rely on others to do it for me. It was something so simple, I should have been able to do myself. I remember I was determined to tie my hair that day and not rely on someone else to do something so trivial. After many attempts, and greatly frustrated, I somehow managed to do it (albeit not very neatly). I was elated! It was a small triumph, but I was ecstatic! It was a small win that I could celebrate. Over the years, I have gotten better at tying my hair into a ponytail, and as I have been saying for many years now, "practice makes permanent."

I don't believe in perfect. Even when you think you have mastered something or created something to the best of your ability, I believe there is always room for improvement. Think about work processes, systems, products, and services. Even when they are launched and should be the best that they can be, there is always a newer, better version launched later that is faster, makes your job easier, provides better service to the customer, and so on.

My journey of change and transformation began when I looked back and recognised the signs of depression. I am usually a positive person with a determined mindset. I can also be stubborn, which probably helped me during this time. I remember times when I felt like I was drifting down a spiral but I would give myself a quick pep talk, chastise myself, and remind myself I was still alive. I could still walk, talk, and function. I had my mental and physical capacity, although slightly limited. Other than that, I was grateful. We often forget about the things we have, focussing on what we don't. Having an attitude of gratitude shifts your focus to the positive. I learned that appreciating what we do have far outweighs lamenting what we don't have. I apply the following two principles every day. They help me when I am faced with life's challenges:

1. Celebrate wins, especially the small wins.
2. Have an attitude of gratitude.

As you will agree, these observances or lessons are not radical or new. Neither are they rocket science. But they are proven. Over the following pages, I will share stories of people dear to me who have applied these lessons to overcome challenges, face their fears, and rise.

There are rational fears that keep us safe—for example, being struck by lightning when swimming during a summer thunderstorm (it happens here in Australia)—and there are irrational fears, like being afraid to go to the dentist for your annual check-up. In the long run, if you continue to avoid doing the latter, you will put your oral health and hygiene at risk. I am not an expert on any of the topics I discuss in the following pages.

This book is a vehicle for me to share the story of my learning journey over a lifetime of observances and experiences. I share my story in the hope it may help anyone reading it and prompt them to go deeper into their own learning journey.

The first of these observances relates to my beloved late grandma. Following this, I will share observances relating to my mum, followed by my own learnings.

Love is what we are born with. Fear is what we have learned here. The spiritual journey is the unlearning of fear and the acceptance of love back in our hearts.

–Marianne Williamson

A lady of grace and exquisite beauty. A loving mother, grandmother, and great-grandmother

𝓜y grandmother was the oldest girl of ten children. According to my mother, my grandmother has five younger sisters and four brothers—a total of six girls and four boys (including twins) in my grandmother's immediate family. My grandmother was born in North Vietnam in 1922 and lived a long life, to the grand age of ninety-six. My grandmother experienced much sadness and loss in her long and sometimes difficult life.

Grandma at age 59

Despite this, she was one of the happiest, generous, compassionate, cheekiest, and most joyful person I knew! My fondest memories of my grandmother are joyful, mischievous, happy, and loving. I was deeply affected by her passing in September 2018, after she succumbed to pneumonia. My grandmother passed away a day before my wedding anniversary, so it is one of three dates that week that hold a special significance for me. I experienced the worst anxiety and depression the following months after her death, and I sought assistance, which helped immensely. It also triggered the realisation of who I need to surround myself with, who I should have in my life, and who

I needed to purge—a "people detox." I was finally realising the importance of who you should surround yourself with.

The following paragraphs below are my remembrance of my Grandma, which I read at her funeral:

> Grandma was and is a beautiful soul. She radiated beauty from the inside out. Grandma was understated but elegant.
>
> Cheeky, loving and kind, tolerant, compassionate, caring, feisty, courageous, independent, stubborn, and brave. Grandma was all these things and much more. Grandma always had spirit, and this has passed onto her daughter, granddaughters, and great-granddaughter.
>
> When Grandma stayed with my family, she loved to sit just outside on our front doorstep—getting a bit of sun, watching the day unfold. I've found it is my favourite spot, and I sit there any morning I am able to—to soak up the morning sun and watch the world wake up.
>
> Grandma was very much a part of our lives and still is. She lives on in our hearts and memories. Grandma is sorely missed and deeply loved—we miss her laughter, her smile, and her kind words. May she watch over us now and join her beloved sons and husband who passed away before her.

As I write this, I am in tears again, but not the uncontrollable sobs that I had at her funeral. I also realised I made a mistake. I should have written, "And join her beloved children" because my grandmother also lost a daughter before she had my mother. She had lost sons as well—the brother my mum grew up with, along with an older brother. Despite her hardships, my grandmother was a joyful and loving woman. She lost children due to war and illness, but she never lost her spirit. It may have diminished a little each time, but she was always a fighter.

My grandmother told us about how she had been separated from her family because of the separation of North and South Vietnam. My mum does not remember much about her uncles and aunties growing up because of this; however, I remember my mum saying one of her uncles was a pilot. So, it is safe to conclude that one of my grandmother's brothers became a pilot. My grandmother's father was an engineer and owned his own business, which meant his family was adequately provided for. My mum told me that my grandmother's father was firm but fair. He was a generous and loving man, often teaching his children and grandchildren to be generous to those less fortunate.

Looking back at the limited number of photos we have of my grandmother as a girl and young woman, you can see she was a lady with elegance and great taste. She was well-dressed, smiling, and looked happy. I learned from my grandma not only by what she said but also by her actions. She was a generous person—generous with her love, time, and possessions. My grandma would remind us that we can't take things with us when we die, so it is better to share and enjoy them with people we love and care about now—in the present. As she was someone who had lost everything in the war, material possessions did not impress her greatly. Granted, my grandmother liked nice things and was an elegant lady with great taste; however, these things did not consume her. She did not need material possessions to be happy.

Grandma in the woods

As a result of her upbringing, my grandmother learned to be firm but fair from her father. Those who are unfamiliar with the Asian culture might assume my grandmother was not kind or loving to her daughter, my mum. However, when you hear my mum talk about how much her mother taught her and loved her, as she reveals the things her mother did for her, you come to realise what you see at any point in time never reveals the true extent of any situation. When it comes to family, there is so much beneath the surface, especially when cultures, traditions, generations, and expectations come into play. This is a topic that requires a whole other discussion.

Back to my grandmother. She loved her daughter, my mum, dearly, despite stating her preference for males over females, as was common with older Asian generations. My grandmother always talked about and praised her boys, her grandsons, our partners, and their sons, as well as our male friends when we introduced them to her. Basically, she was fond of anyone who happened to be male. We all took it in good humour, given her age. We accepted this about her even though we didn't agree with it. We knew it was what she grew up with and was her sphere of reference. Our love and acceptance of my grandmother—faults and all, was due to the unconditional love she showed to her daughter and her granddaughters (myself and my siblings). She was surrounded by females, and even though we were all different, she accepted us for who we were, even when we got under each other's skin!

My mother knew how it felt growing up with her older brother, bearing the brunt of favouritism towards him. Because of her experience, my mother raised us without the mindset of male favouritism. However, I learned that my mother was her grandfather's favourite, being the only girl, and could never seem to get in serious trouble with him, so I guess that evened things out. An example of how my grandmother showed her preference to males was the allocation of food. She would always make sure the boys had plenty of food to eat and would ask us girls to make sure the boys ate. One time, when one of my male friends, Bill, was visiting, she kept giving me our homemade spring rolls to feed him (along with some freshly cooked prawns). I said to her in Vietnamese, "It's okay, Grandma. I think he's had enough," as she couldn't speak much English.

She replied, "But he keeps eating them when you give them to him!"

My friend advised me at a later date that he was very full yet didn't want to be rude and offend my grandmother, so he kept eating the food she offered. Even through this small gesture, my grandmother displayed her generosity. Bill and I caught up in

January 2020, and he reminded me of this as we were about to have lunch together. We both remembered it with fondness and humour.

Our family often came together around food. My grandmother's favourite food was spring rolls and pretty much anything that was fried. One of my grandmother's quick snack foods, which she taught me to make, was fried vermicelli noodles. The noodles are prepared in the usual way so they are white and fluffy, and then my grandmother would advise me to get a frypan, covering the base with oil. Then she would ask me to take a small portion of noodles and place them into the frypan— enough to cover the base and about 1 cm thick. They would be placed in there and fried until the base was golden brown and the noodles stuck together. We would then place them onto a plate and, in the frypan, add a little extra oil, and fry some shallots. After adding a little sugar and salt, we added the shallots to soy sauce and poured them over the noodles, they were ready to eat—a quick, satisfying, crunchy little snack! We learned later on through my grandmother's regular health check-up that she had high cholesterol and should avoid fried food. Our family doctor advised us that my grandmother should consume fried food in moderation. The issue with this was that with all of us at work and school during the day, my grandmother, being able-bodied until her early 90s, was able to cook and fry whatever she pleased. When my grandmother reached her early 90s, my mother took her to the family doctor for a check-up, concerned at the amount of fried foods she was consuming. My mother was limiting the fried food she cooked at home and limiting the types of foods my grandmother liked to fry so my grandmother would have healthier options. My mum expressed this concern to the doctor, and he replied, "Your mother is ninety-two years old. She's lived a long life. Let her enjoy her life a little now." My grandmother even had the doctor on her side! Her joyful countenance was infectious despite the language barrier.

Despite losing a lot over the course of her life, she also gained. My grandmother never lost her generous spirit and gratitude for being alive, surrounded with family and friends. She would often remind us to be grateful for the food we had, the roof over our heads, and the ability to provide for ourselves. Her attitude was infectious. She enjoyed sharing with her family, friends, and loved ones. My grandma would remind us to be grateful for what we had and not to wish for what others had. She celebrated the fact that she was finally able to be reunited with her daughter (my mother) after the Vietnam War separated them and to live in a country of opportunity. She celebrated having food to eat, clothes to wear, a bed to sleep in, and a roof over her head to keep her warm and dry. My grandma was ever grateful to be surrounded by family and friends, and was always happiest when surrounded by family. She lost a lot in the Vietnam War, not just possessions, and this taught me not to cling to material things. My grandmother advised me that material possessions may make you happy temporarily, but having family and people who care about you is most important. People are not replaceable; however, material possessions can be.

My grandmother knew about loss. She lost a daughter before my mum was born. My mum would have had an older sister; however, when her sister was around eight or nine years old, she complained of a headache and went upstairs to lie down. When my grandmother went to check on her, she had passed away. My mum explained that she had had an aneurism that burst, causing her death. My mum longed for a sister growing up in a house full of boys and always reminds my sisters and me how lucky we are to have each other.

My mum also explained how my grandmother lost a son in World War II as well as the brother she had grown up with after the Vietnam War. My mum advised her brother, my uncle, when he was released from the prisoner of war camp and came home to his family, that they were all relieved he was alive and happy to be reunited. When I met my cousin (his son) for the first time, he told me about the night his father passed away. This was different for some reason. He said his dad had gone upstairs to sleep and everyone else had stayed downstairs to let him get a good night's sleep. They would usually sleep together upstairs. His mum would often check on his dad, but for some reason, she didn't that night he passed away during his sleep. It was revealed my uncle passed away due to a heart attack. I remember as a teenager when my mum received news of her brother's death; she was beside herself with grief and felt helpless being in Australia, unable to help other than financially and from a distance. Seeing my mum's grief, I can't even begin to imagine how my grandmother felt. After the relief of welcoming her son home, she would now mourn his passing a short while after he had returned. Now a parent myself, I can't imagine how I would feel if I lost my daughter, yet my grandmother lost three children during her lifetime. You will be familiar with the saying "No parent should have to bury their children." When you imagine how a parent would feel, your heart goes out to them. My grandmother did have her moments when she would be quiet, reflective, and quite sad. My grandma did not fully enjoy the month of December or the Christmas season, because it reminded her of her children's deaths. It was a hard time for her. She still would enjoy the time she spent with us, but there were times when she would withdraw. Thankfully, my mum explained the reason so we would understand.

My mum applied for sponsorship of my grandmother. When it was finally granted, she was reunited with my mother around November 1985. My grandmother was a bundle of joy even after her first long solo flight to a strange country, where she would start her new life—at the age of sixty-nine! She couldn't speak English, and she had endured a solo flight across continents, but that didn't prevent her from being joyful when reunited with her daughter after so many years. The day my grandmother arrived in Australia was the first day I feel we officially met. The last time she had seen me was when my parents left Vietnam when I was just a year old—still a baby. She had not seen me since that day. I remember my grandmother being happy and cheerful even though she must have been very tired after travelling from Vietnam to Australia. My grandma lived with our family during my teenage years, and for many years after I moved out of home at age twenty-one.

I fondly remember my grandma's joy when she and her friend would go to the local club for lunch and a play on the poker machines after receiving their weekly allowance. Neither of them could speak English well, but it didn't stop them; they were clever and cunning! One day, out of the blue, my grandma asked me if I could write down our address and phone number for her on a piece of paper in clear, large writing. When I asked her why she needed it, she explained it was in case of an emergency. That sounded rational to me (a teenager, mind you), so I wrote it clearly and in large hand so she could practise and read it. Apparently, her friend had asked the same from her grandchildren! Later, we found out the real reason for this request was because my grandmother and her friend would call for a taxi, go to the local club together, have their fun, and then catch a taxi back home by showing the taxi driver their addresses. Ingenious! All the while, we were at school and work, unaware these antics were taking place. Looking back, I am grateful no one took advantage of two elderly ladies with money in their pockets and a limited vocabulary. The two of them had many adventures together, one time even ending up at the Sydney Opera House, where they called her friend's son to come and pick them up at the white "shell" house in the city. Joyful, indeed!

Other fond memories of my grandmother being joyful are the times she spent with her great-grandchildren. She would often be laughing and singing with them, and my daughter and her cousins would be laughing and playing along with their great grandmother. I have observed there is no language barrier when it comes to love and play—they are evident despite language and cultural differences. My grandmother was a testament to this. None of her great-grandchildren could speak Vietnamese to her, and she was unable to converse in English to them, but she always showed them love and expressed it in her actions.

Grandma with my daughter on her third birthday

I remember my grandma being happiest with her family around her. She enjoyed being with her grandchildren and great-grandchildren, playing with them and finding ways to amuse my daughter and her cousins despite the language barrier. My grandmother faced many challenges and changes in her life, going from a life full of abundance to losing everything in the war—her possessions, her family, and her children—to being reunited in a foreign country with her only daughter. At the age of sixty-nine, she had to adjust to a new culture, a new family, and new living arrangements. My grandma learned to adapt to change and transformed many times over her lifetime, yet even through these challenges—many of them momentous changes—she managed to enjoy life, be grateful, be joyful, and have a generous spirit that lives on in her daughter, granddaughters, and great-granddaughters. She will forever be in my heart. This is how her memory will live on for her great-granddaughter, my daughter, who was fortunate to have known her great-grandmother. I remind my daughter how lucky she is to have known her great-grandmother; some children don't even get to know their grandparents let alone their great-grandparents. My daughter was twelve years old when my grandmother passed away, so she has been blessed to have her in her life and be at an age when she can remember her great-grandmother.

Grandma's cheeky smile (lady with handbag draped over right arm)

My grandmother lived a challenging yet long life, one that I could never imagine, living through war and rebuilding her life many times. My grandmother was a fighter who had to restart her life because of the Vietnam War. She was entrepreneurial and worked selling street food to provide herself with an income. It was hard work, but it also provided some independence, something my mother taught my sisters and I to achieve. Independence was important to my grandmother and my mum. They valued hard work and determination. This enabled them to appreciate what they had worked for to provide for themselves and their family. Despite the hardship she experienced, my grandmother was a kind, loving, and joyful soul. Her cheeky smile has been passed down through

Grandma as a young lady

the generations to her daughter, granddaughters, and great-granddaughters. You can see this smile in the photo above. When I saw it, I realised this is the same smile my mum, sisters, niece, and daughter all have, and it is a lovely reminder that my grandmother lives on in all of us. My grandmother lives on forever—in our lives, our hearts, and our spirit. I believe she watches over us, providing her love and protection. My grandmother is ever present in my family's life, and I feel her presence in many things—the rain, dragonflies, food and special occasions—sometimes unexpected but always welcome. Her presence provides much fondness—a feeling that she is still looking after her family, blessing us with her presence. I feel she is one of my guardian angels.

My Mother: My Rock, My Guide, and My Only Living Guardian Angel

∘∙∘

*M*y mother is alive and well. She has always looked after me, and I feel she is my only living guardian angel. My mother has taught me so much and continues to teach me—in her words, her actions, her kindness, and her empathy towards others. At times, people take advantage of these traits, yet my mother says treating someone with kindness is better than lowering your standards. She teaches me to treat others how I would like to be treated, and this is not always easy,

My gorgeous mother as a young adult

especially if the other person isn't reciprocating my kindness! I have learned that it's better to be kind and learn when you shouldn't tolerate less from others. You learn you cannot help everyone and not everyone appreciates your kindness. However, this is no excuse not to be kind. Your actions are a reflection of you and what you would like to receive. As I have often stated, "The energy you give out is what comes back to you." Learning this can be difficult depending on how people may treat you. However, throughout my life, I have found it to be true. If you give out love and kindness, you receive it back in return. If you radiate negativity, then you receive it in return. Learning and applying this principle ensures you radiate the energy you would like to receive.

From a young age, my mother always said to me, "You never stop learning." She continues to tell me this even now. My mother instilled a mindset of learning, curiosity, and thirst for knowledge. For as long as I can remember, my mum has consistently tried new things—sometimes with much success and sometimes not so much. However, she always learned something from the experience. My mum would try something as simple as cooking a new recipe or trying a new food product to something as complex as changing jobs. When I was growing up, my mum worked in a laundromat in Mount St. Margaret Hospital, interpreting school correspondence for a local primary school and being part of the process to make CDs, DVDs, and Blu-Ray discs in Sony Music. My mother didn't get to finish high school in Vietnam, yet she learns quickly and is open to learning something new. To this day, my mum will still bring me some new biscuit or chocolate, ask if I have tried it, and give me some to try. Sometimes she gives it to me because she tried it herself and didn't like it; other times, because she liked it so much, she wanted to share the joy!

Facing change with an open mind and the flexibility to learn from any experience has helped my mum get through times of adversity. There are some experiences which have taken her longer to bounce back from, yet she has rebounded from others with ease. I feel this is due to how she allows herself to process, digest, and learn from the experience. Sometimes the lesson is harder for her to learn, so it takes her longer to get through it, and other times, she is able to shake it off and move forward quickly. My mother had a great job in Vietnam working for the Bank of America. She learned English by listening and watching people talking with each other and listening to Western music. She grew up listening to the

Beatles, Diana Ross, Helen Reddy, Boney M, and much more. My mother loved music of all genres, and to this day, she blasts music on her stereo at home and in her car. I remember growing up listening to all types of music. As a result, I grew up loving all genres of music, which I've passed onto my daughter. This mindset of continuous learning is also a great way to cope with change and the challenges that relate to the change. I have found it helps to be flexible and open to finding the opportunity in such challenges.

Having an open, curious mindset allows you to learn new things, be open to change, and face any challenges that come with that change. Fear is something that my mother has had to face many times in her life—the Vietnam war, leaving her homeland, nearly losing her firstborn, relocating to another country without any immediate family, and then migrating to another country (which she initially thought was Austria in Europe!). Our family migrated to Australia in the early 1970s when I was only eighteen months old. We moved here so we could be reunited with my father's side of the family. His mum, sister, and younger brother were already in Australia. It's a decision that my mum is ever grateful for to this day. My mum truly believes Australia is a lucky country because it has given her the opportunity to live a relatively comfortable life and raise her family in a country that provides many opportunities which would have been unavailable had we stayed in Vietnam. My mum also practises an attitude of gratitude, remembering where she has been and the opportunities she has been provided since coming to Australia—the "Lucky Country." My mum believes it is lucky because we have access to clean water, fresh fruit and vegetables, education, and employment. She believes if you work hard, apply yourself, and make the most of your opportunities, you can have a happy, comfortable life. My mum reminds me that we are lucky to have each other to help and care for and be there to support each other. This is worth more to her than any material possessions. My mum is grateful for her family and that she has her family to share her life with.

Throughout all the change in her life, my mum retained her inner strength, a resilience she herself might not be aware of. However, she has faced and overcome many challenges, and because of her inner strength, she continues to do so. My mum has a lot of self-reliance and determination and uses these strengths to get her through even the most daunting times. My mother created this life for herself and her family based on what she knew would be best for herself and her family. She did not have the luxury of her family or good friends around her as she built her new life. She learned to rely on herself and often the good grace of strangers she met along the way, some of whom became friends. I feel we often take for granted our friends, family, and loved ones, and I wonder how we would have coped in my mother's situation. It's an experience that not many of us have ever or ever will experience. I am grateful my mother is part of my daughter's life. She learns from her grandmother, and their relationship is a special bond. My daughter has heard of the hardships her grandmother and great grandmother have overcome, which I feel helps her understand her history.

My mother's gratefulness for the opportunity to live a better life is not lost on her and she constantly reminds us of her gratitude. She creates her own happiness and even though, at times life does get her down, her spark is always there in her stories, laughter and love towards her family. My mum loves wearing vibrant colours and doing what she enjoys (even if it means not doing much and sleeping in). She teaches us to be self-reliant and independent so we can take care of ourselves and teach our children to do the same. Self-reliance provides you with the power to create a life you can be proud of. I have learned it is not something that you rely on other people to measure. It is how your life looks to you. Success means many things to many people; however, through self-reliance, *your* measure of success is most important. I found a quote that resonates:

> Work hard in silence, let your success be your noise.
> —Frank Ocean

I read this quote without knowing who Frank Ocean was (born Christopher Edwin Cooksey). Based on what I found on Wikipedia, he is an American songwriter, record producer, and photographer. Without being distracted by who the quote is attributed to, I often find quotes that resonate with me and will research their sources if I am unfamiliar with them. It often helps to understand the influences in their life that may have led them to craft their statement. As I mentioned earlier, everyone has a story, and so does Frank Ocean, so please feel free to research and read about what has been documented about his life if this interests you. The quote resonates with me because of the interpretation I take from this: your success is not defined by anyone or anything but yourself. Think about how you measure your success. Often, people respond by listing material things. However, once you have obtained them, what else is there? My mother and grandmother both viewed material possessions as just that, nothing more, nothing less. They both taught me to value my things and to look after them. However, their collective attitude was "You come into the earth with nothing. You also leave with nothing." This perspective has rubbed off on me, and I am teaching my daughter the same

Yes, while we like to have nice things, we are mindful of the fact that they are just that, *things*. They do not define who we are or our happiness. If we lose something dear to us, we may be upset, but the memories attached to them and the sentiment remain. This became more evident for me when my mother's house was broken into twice. She lost all the lovely gifts we had bought for her over the years. Now my mum says to me that she doesn't buy expensive things because of this and enjoys what she has, which is still a lot more than some people. This has helped me change my mindset towards material possessions, and I am very grateful my mum was not home during both burglaries and was not harmed. I feel losing my mum would be worse than losing all the things that were stolen from her house. My grandfather said to my mum while she was growing up, "You are rich when you are rich in your heart." This is something my mum remembers with fondness about her grandfather, and she has passed the same philosophy to me.

My mum trying a gorgeous pink sapphire necklace at Tiffany's but did not purchase—it was enough to try it on and enjoy the moment.

The fear we attach to losing something, someone, or someplace we hold dear makes us place a higher value on that item than it warrants. My mother's experience has slowly transformed my way of thinking. It is fine to value nice things, people, places, and what they provide; however, learning to let go and enjoy the lesson or the blessing they bring into your life provides the most value. There have been times when I felt my mother was not living her best life. I would take time to reflect in these moments so I could understand and empathise. My mum continues to live despite experiencing heartbreak, death, and loss. She continues to display and encourage joy, gratitude, and happiness. I have written a series of three blog posts to record her story for my daughter, family, and friends to read and share the experience and hopefully convey the emotions of her story when she fled her birth country. They also preserve a bit of our family history for future generations. If you would like to read them, please click on the links below:

The Journey Begins

I mentioned in a previous post that I would document my story which is a recollection of my Mother's story which now also forms part of my daughter's story. Here is the beginning of my story, I've documented the recollection of my mum's memories so I hope to do her story justice.

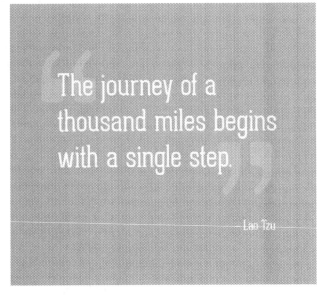

The journey of a thousand miles begins with a single step.

— Lao Tzu

My story starts with the fall of Saigon, 30 April 1975. My mum remembers the confusion and desperation of people who didn't know what was happening, what they should do or where they should go. I was 11 months old and my mum, who was a former US employee for the CPA (Central Purchasing Agency) went with a servant to the US Embassy to see if she and her family could be taken out of the country. She was informed that there was a bus that would take former and current employees with their immediate families but they had to leave straight away. My mum was still waiting for her husband, my dad, to return home from his army compound. As a result, my mum didn't leave on that bus – she also didn't want to leave without her extended family – her mother, brother and his family.

My mum made the decision to go home. She and her servant took a bus back home and waited for my dad to return, she wasn't sure when he would arrive. My mum said that the Vietnamese President had surrendered so the soldiers of the South Vietnamese army had laid down their weapons. All commanders sent soldiers home, so my dad left his compound and went home to collect my mum and I. My mum said she remembers that people were running everywhere; they didn't know what was going to happen or where to go - it was an atmosphere of chaos and confusion. People just knew they wanted to leave. My parents were of the same mind, they wanted to try and find a way out of the country as fast as they could. My mum said that we all jumped onto a Honda motorbike to get to a meeting place organised by my mum's uncle. My mum's Uncle was in the Air force and had informed them to be at a certain location – where a helicopter would arrive to take them out by air. They had to get to the roof of the building so they could board the helicopter. When my parents arrived, there were too many people, they could not get onto the roof and the crowd were almost tipping the helicopter over so it had to leave. Another escape attempt foiled.

Hugh Van Es's iconic image of a helicopter rescue on a Saigon rooftop

My mum said that my dad's best man had advised him to go to the seaside and see if there was any chance to escape by sea. My parents set out to the Navy compound/ dock in Saigon. When they arrived, they saw that it too was very crowded and full of people. There were Navy ships bringing people back from Da Nang to Saigon as there was a US base in Da Nang. There were people scrambling to get on board the ships that were returning as soon as it had reached the dock. The men would climb on board and then pull their wives and children on afterwards. As a result, my mum said that many people fell into the water. My dad got on board a ship and pulled my mum who was carrying me, onto the ship. The servant girl who had come along, threw my mum a bag with some clothes, nappies and baby formula but didn't get on board. My mum thinks she wanted to go back to her own family. She never saw her again.

My mum said that there were so many people already on the ship but more were still scrambling to get on board. The Navy Commander was on board the ship my parents had scrambled onto. He also had his family on board, but what people weren't aware of, was that the ship wasn't working - people just scrambled on board any ship, they were desperate to leave Saigon. The Navy Commander and his team worked to get the engine started. My mum said that luckily, they were able to fix the ship's engine and when it started, everyone cheered! My mum said she didn't know how many people were on the ship, she guessed hundreds! She said they all sat with their legs crossed and drawn up to their chests. My mum also had me on her lap so it was very uncomfortable and cramped. In hindsight, my mum now realises that she had to escape without her extended family anyway, to give her immediate family a chance of survival.

Refugees scrambling on board a ship that will evacuate them - image www.rogerogreeen.com

When the ship left the dock, my mum said that everyone thought that the ship was going from one side of the Mekong River to the other – like a ferry service. Little did they realise that it was going out to sea. My mum said that the captain of the ship used a black tarpaulin to cover and hide the crowds of people on the ship on the top deck so that it would not be suspected of anything other than a Navy ship. This way, when communist helicopters flew overhead, they would not see the people crowded on board. Most people were taking a chance by getting on this ship. They felt it was better to take a chance to escape even if it meant drowning. People thought it would be better to die in the river than live under communist rule.

My mum said that after some time, people heard that they were at open sea. The Navy ship rescued a lot of fishing boats that had fled to sea. My mum said at one point, there were so many people on board that the ship was taking on water. All able men had to bail out the water. During the course of the journey, my mum said that they were allowed to quickly stretch their legs then crouch back into position so everyone could fit. Each family was given a handful of rice as all other food and water had been depleted. The only water that became available after the fresh water ran out was sea water. My mum said so many people got very sick and everyone became quite smelly. Their clothes had turned black due to the dirt and grease on the ship. She said that she remembers people would go around and touch you on the shoulder and if you made no noise, you were thought to be dead. When this happened, my mum said people were thrown overboard so there would be more space on board the ship. My mum said she was tapped on the shoulder and asked if she was still alive. My mum answered 'Yes'. She did not want to be thrown overboard.

This is the beginning of the journey for my parents and I - this is our story. I will continue the story once I have finished editing the next part of our journey. It's an amazing story and not unlike other refugees at the time. I'm glad to finally be documenting this for my own benefit as well as my daughter's. I hope it sparks curiosity to find out your story so you are able to share it with friends and loved ones too.

The Journey Continues...

Here is the next part of My story - my mum's memories become a bit scattered but I have captured it to the best of my ability. Let's continue the journey to see where it leads us...

Our journey continues

My mum remembers that on the 8th day at sea, A US Navy carrier ship rescued them - they were near Subic Bay, Phillipines. She remembers that someone on the US Navy ship asked if anyone could speak English and as my mum had worked for the US, CPA she just said "Help Us." The US Navy carrier ship took them in and gave everyone some food and water. Everyone on board the Vietnamese navy ship had to line up to get onto the US Carrier ship so that doctors and helpers could assist you once you were on board. My mum was in a state of distress and left the line because I had fallen gravely ill. The US Officer, pointed his gun at my mum and ordered her back into line. My mum said sat just down crying and said "My baby's dying".

The US Officer, hearing my mum speak English, looked at me in her arms and asked my mum "You talk?". My mum answered "Yes, I can talk." The officer asked my mum to follow him, he took her to the doctor so he could examine me straight away. My mum feels that if she had stayed in line then she would have lost me. The doctor placed me in the hospital as I was diagnosed with severe diarrhoea.

My mum became the translator for the Vietnamese people and the US army. The captain would ask my mum "You talk, okay?". My mum would agree and say "Yes, I talk." The officers handed out canned food (peaches, SPAM, etc) for the refugees to eat. The people would ask my mum if the food was alright to eat, she would look at the pictures on the cans and explain if it contained fruit or meat, etc so they could eat it. They would encourage each other to eat, especially my mum as she found difficulty eating after being near starvation but people encouraged my mum to eat. They said to my mum that she must eat otherwise she would be thrown into the sea! This was based on their experience on board the ship they had been on when they left Vietnam.

At first, my mum said there was some issue with the Philippine Government, they wouldn't allow the refugees to be brought into the country. My mum wasn't aware of what the issue(s) were but they were eventually resolved and they were allowed to be brought into the Philippines. *

* I did a bit of research and found this link that details the rescue of the Vietnamese refugees and the reason for the delay in coming to shore:

http://www.npr.org/2010/09/01/129578263/at-war-s-end-u-s-ship-rescued-south-vietnam-s-navy

Welcome sign at the entrance to the base.

Once they were allowed to be brought into the Philippines, temporary accommodation was set up for the refugees in the holiday area in Subic Bay, that was used by the Commanders and their families when on leave. My mum said that the Vietnamese refugees felt so lucky to be staying there – to them it was pure luxury and felt like 5-star accommodation compared to what they had just been through! My mum said, thinking back, it was probably basic holiday accommodation – it was clean, comfortable and had all the basics but to them it felt like they were in heaven!

My mum said she remembers having food, being able to watch movies and listen to live music. She said that if you had your own money, then you were able to go to the supermarket that was available there and purchase your own items. My mum had no money, just the clothes and little jewellery she had when she jumped aboard the ship. My mum said she traded her jewellery with the cleaner for food – apples, oranges, noodles. She said she traded her Rolex watch for $5 US dollars! She had no idea of the value of her jewellery. She was just concerned about being able to could purchase food, baby formula and cigarettes for my dad. My mum relayed a funny story about the baby formula she had bought for me. She said that initially she didn't realise that she needed to mix the formula with water so ended up scooping it in powdered form and feeding it to me!

My mum said that the refugees were sanctioned into different areas and categorised by colour eg Families with young children in red area, families without children in blue area, etc. There were 3 families in each of the holiday homes and refugees were given 3 meals a day as well as clothes while they were staying at the holiday accommodation in Subic Bay *.

* I found this small piece of information regarding the Vietnamese refugees taken in at Subic Bay under the heading Vietnam War, as it became a large processing area for the Vietnamese refugees: https://en.wikipedia.org/wiki/U.S._Naval_Base_Subic_Bay

So that details part 2 of Our Story, to be continued at another time. A lot changed for my parents & I once we left our birth country, yet there are more changes ahead...

Journey into the unknown

This is the final leg of My Story, the final part of my family's journey from Vietnam...

Once I was well enough, my mum said that we were transported to a temporary refugee camp on Guam island, then moved to Wake island and eventually to California in the United States of America. Once in America, the Red Cross became involved and would organise for a church/ community to sponsor a refugee family to help them settle into their new life in America, Canada or France. My mum volunteered with the Red Cross to assist her in locating other family members. My mum said she became friendly with one of the ladies who worked for the Red Cross, who spoke French. My mum's French was very limited but they were able to communicate through my father who was more fluent in French. He said that he also had family overseas, so the Red Cross helped in finding my father's family too.

My mum also had met up with a cousin (my uncle) in the refugee camp in the Philippines but he was placed in a different area of the camp, as he was an ex-army officer and single. My mum became separated from her cousin and didn't know how to find him. My mum found out later that he had written her a letter which was delivered by the Red cross to the refugee camp - but because she was moved, she never received the letter. He had written to inform her that he had gotten to America and where to find him. The Red Cross informed my mum that her cousin had been sponsored and was now settled in America. They advised my mum to choose a sponsor that was available from the bulletin board in their office if she wanted to leave the refugee camp.

My mum had memorised her sister-in-law's address, who was at the time residing in Indonesia with her husband and family. At that time, my uncle was the Australian Ambassador in Indonesia. My mum sent a telegram to my Aunty to inform her that we had reached the United States of America. She didn't know how to say 'sister-in-law' in French so told the Red Cross Volunteer that she was her 'cousine'. However, when the telegram was sent, it stated my mum and family were in the US, it did not include my father's name so my Aunty assumed that only my mum and I had escaped Vietnam. Apparently my Aunty had sent a telegram advising us to stay in the US, but my mum never received it.

My mum said she surveyed the board and the Red Cross had organised it to display and indicate the church community that would sponsor either an individual or family of 3, 5, etc. They were also listed by country – United States, Canada, France. My mum said she had to review them and decide which group she wanted to be sponsored by and advise the Red

Cross. The Red Cross and the US Government would then organise for the church community ie a family from that church community to sponsor us.

Teams of Red Cross nurses, staff and volunteers worked around the clock greeting the exhausted children and providing them with nursing care as they made their way to new homes in America.

www.redcross.org

My mum, not knowing that there were different Christian denominations, just chose any church group, which turned out to be a Lutheran church. My mum was only aware of the Roman Catholic church, as was her experience in Vietnam so didn't realise that it would be different. However, when she attended mass, she realised that it was. She asked the Lutheran Pastor if she could attend Catholic mass instead.

The family who sponsored our family lived in South Dakota so we were settled there to be close to them. They advised my parents that they needed to find employment to help them start a life. My dad found a job first, although my mum can't recall where! My mum contacted one of the Vietnamese Captains whose phone number she had memorised to ask him about finding a job. My mum said the Captain spoke to someone in the church asking them to assist my mum in finding employment. My mum was taken to the employment office and found a job in office admin, where she completed filing and typing.

What my mum wasn't aware of was that the Red Cross had also found my dad's family overseas. The Red Cross had located my dad's family in Australia – his mum, and a younger brother and sister. My mum didn't know where Australia was at the time and asked 'Where is Australia?' Even though she was unsure of where we would be going, she thought it would be better for me to be surrounded by a Grandmother, Aunty and Uncle so she made the decision to go to Australia. As it was my dad's mother who had been located, this was higher priority and a stronger connection than my mum's 'cousine' even though it was my dad's older sister. So, as a result, my Grandmother's telegram took precedence. The telegram from my Grandmother stated that she would like her son & granddaughter to come and live in Australia.

I believe everyone has a story and that sharing your story helps the healing process, if this is what is required. It can be cathartic and trigger a process of transformation. As I have mentioned, these learnings I am sharing are not fresh and new; however, they are relevant and proven based on my observances of my grandmother and mother's experiences. I hope I spark your own journey and trigger your curiosity to learn. Being even a small part of your transformation is a reward in itself. My mother and my grandmother are important aspects of my life, my family's life, and our shared history. Learning from their lives, trials, and triumphs enables me to live my best life, and I hope to impart the same knowledge to my daughter. I also hope to impart these learnings to you, dear reader.

My mum continues to inspire and motivate me to become a better person. She has been involved with charities for as long as I can remember. When I was younger, we would often accompany my mum when she volunteered at the Salvation Army to sort through donated goods. She reminds me to be grateful for what we have and to give to those in need. She recalls that we were once in a position of need and received help when we needed it from these charities. Now, we are in a position to help others, so it is our way of giving back. My mum continues her charity works by collecting donations, volunteering, and giving her time and money to other people, churches, and charities. This resonates with me, and I donate, fundraise, volunteer, and give my time when I am able. I feel the act of giving is a reward in itself, and research has proven that altruism leads to a longer, happier life (Post 2005). My mother comes from a line of females who live beyond the age of ninety with relatively good health, so genes and family history are in her favour! Let's hope I will be as fortunate.

My mum has an abundance of empathy. When drought affects the farmers in Australia, she bursts into tears when she hears or sees interviews with farmers who have little to no water and can hardly make a living. My mum recalls the story to me and reminds me that we are lucky we have water, food, and employment so we can provide for our own families' needs. This may seem soft to some people, but few possess such genuine understanding and compassion for people. This demonstrates to me that being kind and compassionate is not soft. It often takes a tough mind and heart to experience the suffering of others and remind yourself to be grateful and help others when you can. My mum continually teaches me to empathise with those in need and show compassion for others. She shared with me a story how her grandfather taught her this lesson when she was young. Here is that story:

My mum was walking with her grandfather, eating corn on a cob, when they passed a beggar on the street. My mum, being a child, threw her half-eaten corn cob to the beggars. She promptly received a reprimand from her grandfather, who said to her, "You pick that up and get a new corn cob to give to this person!" He added, "Would you want a half-eaten corn cob thrown at you. It is dirty now because it fell on the ground. Would you eat a dirty corn cob?" My mum had to go and get a brand-new, uneaten corn cob and give it to the beggar. Her lesson that day: treat other people with the same respect you would give to yourself, your friends, and your family. We are all human, and no matter how different we look on the outside, we are all the same on the inside. My mum often says if you cut her and someone else who is a different race or ethnicity, their blood and hers are the same colour: red. This reminds us we are all part of the human race and should treat each other with respect, kindness, and compassion. We should teach this lesson to our children instead of the division that occurs in the world today.

Collage of photos of mum with my family

As I have mentioned, these learnings are not new and continue to be lessons and strategies we incorporate throughout our lives. I have observed how my grandmother and my mum have demonstrated the application of these lessons in their lives in order to *Face Everything and Rise*. They learned to be flexible, to continuously change and transform throughout their lives to face their challenges. My mum continues to do so, and with empathy, we can learn to understand that everyone must eventually deal with challenges in their lives. It isn't the hardship or challenges that define you; it is how you respond to them and deal with what you have or the cards you are dealt in life. Change is a constant. We can resist it or work with it. When you think about your life, how many changes have you already faced? Growing up, changing schools, moving house, learning to drive, changing jobs and relationships—all these things and many more are changes we face in our lives, some easier than others. In most cases, it is not the change that is difficult or painful; it is our resistance to the change. How can you let go and work with the change? The following is a quote attributed to Buddha which applies to how we can make change easier for ourselves: "Change is never painful. Only resistance to change is painful."

These learnings have helped me and continue to help me throughout my life. I am constantly learning, unlearning, and relearning. It is not easy to unlearn a perspective or behaviour that you have learned from a young age. My grandmother and mother have had to do this many times throughout their lives. My mum is still learning. As I have mentioned, she reminds me, "We never stop learning," and this has proven true throughout my life. We learn about ourselves and others—knowledge, information, behaviours, thoughts, and responses. Sometimes, the unlearning strips back years and years of family expectations and history.

This journey can be eye-opening and challenge your beliefs and expectations. I have found it uncomfortable at times, but this discomfort is the nudge we need to grow. I feel if we remain in the same place, staying comfortable, we do not grow. As the following quote states, "A comfort zone is a beautiful place, but nothing ever grows there." I couldn't find the author or source of this quote, it is listed as "author unknown." I have found this to be true throughout my life by observing my grandmother's and mum's lives. They were both cast out of their comfort zones many times—they grew, changed, transformed, learned to face everything, and rose—often falling and rising again, many times. If you take the first letter of each word of the title of my book, you get the acronym FEAR. We often let fear manifest and give it too much of our time and energy, which results in the fear becoming bigger than it needs to be. My mum and grandmother often did not have time to put their energy to their fear. Their energy was better placed in transitioning and adjusting to the change required in their lives.

I watched an interesting TED Talk by Tim Ferris that provides an interesting perspective. It is titled, "Why You Should Define Your Fears Instead of Your Goals." Please take a moment to watch his talk to see if it resonates with you. I have provided a link in the references section. Please watch it in your free time. It is important to identify and face our fears whenever we can. I face my fears every day, and so does everyone I meet. Every person you meet or who comes into your life is fighting a battle you are not aware of. Letting go of our perceptions and views and accepting others ensures compassion, understanding, and tolerance. Differences will always be present. They do not make people better or right, just different.

Mum and Grandma with grandchildren and great-grandchildren

Laugh, Love, Live!

Life Motto Tattoo

$\mathcal{T}$his part is an introduction to my story and learning journey. I'll start with an explanation of the image above. It is a tattoo I drew and had tattooed onto my left forearm, near my elbow. It is my life motto and one I have been saying and writing in my blogs for the last six or seven years. When I returned from a family holiday to Europe, I felt it was the right tattoo for me at the time. I had always wanted to get a tattoo. However, I could not decide exactly what I wanted, and because of this, I never got one. For some reason, this time, it felt right. I organised to have the tattoo done in a matter of days. In hindsight, there was a different image that I thought would have been my first tattoo. To this day, I still have not tattooed that image.

The family holiday to Europe was something I wanted for a long time, but I never thought it would happen. I had written a letter to my uncle after he passed, promising I would visit my cousin, his son, in England. I didn't know how or when we would be able to travel to England, but I knew we would. The letter was my way of coping with my grief and communicating the unspoken words I couldn't physically say to my uncle but could express in the written form. I felt my uncle's presence after his passing in different aspects of my life—I can't explain how, but I knew it was my uncle's presence. The family holiday occurred a short time after his passing. On this trip, we visited my cousin and his family, and we visited the town where my uncle had spent his childhood—St. Albans. On this trip, we also visited family in Belgium (an aunt and cousins) and travelled to a few places in Europe I had wanted to visit for some time.

The trip to Europe and England became a reality after catching up with my closest friend as we had been thinking of travelling to Japan. My husband was a reluctant traveller, and I mentioned to my friend how he didn't seem eager to travel to Japan. My friend, who had travelled to Japan, started to list the positives of travelling to that country. Then he stopped mid-sentence, turned to me, and asked if I had been to Europe yet.

"No," I replied.

My friend turned to my husband and said, "Take your wife to Europe."

To my surprise, my husband asked him, "When is the best time to travel to Europe?"

The rest is history! I noticed many synchronicities in these days, and I continued to be aware of them instead of dismissing them, especially in the previous twelve months. It seemed that when I put out my intentions to the universe by speaking or thinking them, these intentions became reality. The more I let go of what I felt was holding me back (most often, it was myself), the more would manifest—often involving things I had hoped for and wanted for a long time. These occurrences seemed to happen in quick succession in the previous twelve months. I've learned that we often need to get out of our own way!

I also felt a stronger spiritual nudge after the death of my dear uncle about five years ago, and I noticed synchronicities in greater abundance. These synchronicities included numbers that kept recurring, places we travelled to or visited after speaking or thinking about them, and people who showed up or left my life. Synchronicities also included information that seemed to find its way to me on topics I was interested in but never pursued. Other synchronicities included opportunities for learning and work that seemed to occur that I had been ruminating on—it felt as if the more I put my energy into the learning, change, and transformation I was experiencing, the more they aligned. These synchronicities seemed to be happening more frequently—or perhaps I was just more aware of them. "Synchronicity" is defined as follows on *Dictionary.com*:

1. coincidence in time; contemporaneousness; simultaneousness.
2. the arrangement or treatment of <u>synchronous</u> things or events in conjunction, as in a history.
3. a tabular arrangement of historical events or personages, grouped according to their dates.
4. *Physics, Electricity.* the state of being <u>synchronous</u>.
5. *Psychoanalysis.* the simultaneous occurrence of causally unrelated events and the belief that the simultaneity has meaning beyond mere coincidence.

These symbols, travel experiences, numbers, people moving in or out of my life, and opportunities in work and education all seemed to be linked by coincidence, sometimes completely randomly. Their timing was synchronistic to thoughts or conversations throughout my life; however, they seemed to occur in greater frequency during the previous twelve months. I felt the spiritual nudge become much stronger after my grandmother passed away. I could feel her strong presence in my daily life. As it was previously, as in the case of my uncle's passing, I can't explain what it was like, except I felt a strong presence and knew it was my grandma—there's no other way I can explain it. I know she was there for major decisions in the past year. She was there to help me through some tough times and help me learn the lessons I needed to learn, especially the difficult ones. My grandma was a very strong woman, as is my mother. I have found most strong people I know who have endured tough times display strength and resilience. I like to compare this strength to a diamond; under difficult circumstances shine and hardens into lasting strength and beauty. A diamond doesn't start its journey as a beautiful glittering jewel. It endures extreme heat to bring out its robustness and beauty.

There was also a specific synchronicity that occurred, which I feel without a doubt relates to my grandmother. It was a different opportunity for learning, not formal, as you would receive in a registered learning institution but rather an opportunity to learn more about face reading.

My grandmother was adept at face reading. She taught me the meaning of a few facial features and how they relate to one's character. As a result of face reading, my grandmother was always correct in reading a person—their energy, character, and personality. The facilitator of this course was a chance meeting at a coaching opportunity session I decided to attend after much rumination. I almost did not attend; however, I would gain the benefit of meeting the facilitator of this course and then attending one of her face-reading sessions. It was a three-day course, with the final day culminating on my grandmother's birthday—the first birthday after her passing. I felt it was my grandmother's spirit that led me there. It was an interesting course and confirmed what my grandmother had taught me, opening up helpful knowledge and information, assisting me with the people in my life at the time. Some of them part of my detox during the previous twelve months.

Later, in the Précis, I explain the link between why I associate my grandmother and dragonflies. On the second day of the course, the facilitator mentioned that for some reason, dragonflies were emerging as something of significance to her. I mentioned my grandmother and showed her my dragonfly tattoo I had gotten in her memory. There was also a dragonfly sculpture hanging on her wall I had noticed while attending the course. Once she heard of the significance of the dragonfly, she gave me a green crystal and said it was to help me let go. I wasn't aware I needed to let go of anything, but as I meditated that evening, holding the crystal in my hand, I realised I needed to let go of my grandmother. That evening, while meditating, I felt a tingling sensation in both my legs. I had tears rolling down my face as I spoke to my grandmother and asked her to spread her wings and visit her other loved ones. It was and is the most intense meditation session I have had.

The next day was the final day of the course, and the facilitator decided to finish the session with song. We all stood in a circle, and as the music played, I soon realised it was not only my favourite song but also one of the songs played at my grandmother's funeral. I was unable to control the tears and sobs until the song stopped. The facilitator remarked it was definitely a manifestation of my grandmother's presence. She informed me she seldom ended her sessions with a song, but for some reason that morning, this particular song came to her, so she thought it would be a good idea to play it to wrap up our three-day session. This was a synchronicity I could not ignore. That evening, I visited my grandmother's grave with my family. I spoke to my grandmother and wished her a happy birthday. It is a practice we continue to this day, one way she remains a part of our lives.

During my journey, I have learned that change itself is a process, not stagnant, and transformation happens over time. The many changes, the challenges and choices we face over the course of our lives contribute to this transformation. We may be aware of the change and transformation occurring, be present, and enjoy the process. Or it may happen without our noticing until we reflect and realise how far we've come. As the "new normal" emerges, those reminders enable us to realise the transformation that took (or is taking place). I did not always appreciate and realise the enormity of my gratitude, especially when I was younger. I observed my mother deal with a lot of emotional grief during the losses she experienced in her life, but she is healing. It saddened me watching my mum deal with emotional grief, as it was one of many changes and challenges she overcame. I have learned I can be there for my mum and let her cope in her own way. However, there have been times I wanted her to take some action to alleviate her pain. I forgot that I couldn't force her to do anything she wasn't ready for or didn't want to do and that I could not know what she was feeling. Although it was difficult to witness, I had to let my mum work through her pain her way. I came to realise this is her journey to manage, not mine. I had to learn to be there for my mum when she needed support or just someone to talk to.

As I mentioned in the début, my change and transformation journey commenced after I was involved in a near-death car accident. I don't think I realised it at the time, but in hindsight, I was already changing and evolving. Even now, I am still transforming. Learning is a lifelong journey and one that can surprise you. Those who have experienced a near-death experience may feel a greater sense of gratitude and realise the life they have been gifted is truly that—a gift. The fact that you open your eyes and have the ability to wake up every morning and go about your everyday life is a privilege denied to many. Realising this is paramount to changing your mindset. This is how I view life now: grateful to live my life, have a family to love, and chase our dreams and goals. The simple things in life have become the most important.

After my car accident, I lost my short-term memory for a while due to my head injury. My long-term memory was intact, so I recognised my family and loved ones and remembered other things. Regaining my short-term memory was a blessing, especially for my family, as I no longer repeated things. So often, I would start to say something and would be met with the response, "Yes, you've told us this already." I am grateful not to have suffered brain damage or more serious long-term memory issues resulting from the accident. I have been able to work, study, and raise a family—all things that would prove difficult had there been more adverse consequences of my head injuries.

I mention my accident because it happened in my early twenties. I was young and had moved out of the family home a couple of years prior, graduating with a bachelor's degree from university. I was working full-time and finding my way in the corporate world, hoping my degree would enable me build a successful career. I was beginning to realise the path I wanted to take and what I needed to do to get there. My accident halted that progress for a couple of years as I was out of work for almost a year, recovering from surgery and having weekly physiotherapy sessions to regain the movement in my right hand, fingers, and shoulder. The shoulder was not damaged but had to endure the weight of a metal fixature on my arm, which enabled my elbow fracture and skin grafts to heal. Because of this, I could barely lift my right arm or use my right hand. I had next to no muscle tone due to weight loss. It was a slow, painful process of recovery.

The accident took its toll on me physically, emotionally, and psychologically. There were so many adjustments to be made as I became used to the "new normal." I had to relearn how to do some things differently. My right elbow became fixed, and I can no longer move it. I cannot straighten my right arm, so there are many things I had to relearn how to do with my left hand, as well as adjust how I did things with my right. Neural pathways in my brain changed to accommodate the use of my left hand as my dominant hand. When I was recovering from my accident, my youngest sister, who was around ten years old at the time, told me she would teach me to write with my left hand because she was left-handed—such a sweet gesture from a young child. Luckily, with physiotherapy, I have been able to regain the use of my right hand to write, type, and drive. However, there were still a few things I had to switch over to my left hand, such as brushing my teeth and hair. It took a while, and I am still adjusting even after twenty-two years. It's been an incredible journey, healing from the injuries and shock of having to change the way you do things. I also had to learn to let go of things I knew I would not be able to do myself unassisted, as well as things I would just have to learn to let go. These include doing my own hair, which is why I have had a similar fuss-free hairstyle for many years. Maybe it is time for a change?

I had the fears typical of a young adult in my case, not being able to drive. And if I could drive, would I be able to drive a car with manual transmission? I was also afraid of not being able to exercise the same way, and even something as simple as putting bobby pins in your hair can be daunting if you let it. I found a complete change of mindset was required. I needed to focus on what I *could* do and not what I could no longer do. There was no benefit dwelling on things I could not do, which were outside my control. I had to learn (or relearn) how to do certain things that were in my control. I had to learn to let go of the previous mindset, relearn, and occasionally choose a different mindset. I practise this to this day. Therefore, my journey of transformation is still unfolding. I find we often grow up with preconceived notions from family, society, friends, and peers that we may or may not outgrow. We may find as we get older that we do not fit into these norms. We may have outgrown certain expectations, or we realise we have a different attitude or perspective regarding these notions, which are not right or wrong but are different now. I have found that it is fine to be different. I learned that being different does not mean you are wrong. You may not think the same way about certain things in life and discover that different is okay. I find it often provides food for thought and interesting conversations.

I felt I had always been this way, but after my accident, I had a need to fit in and wanted to be part of a group—any group. My need to fit in and be accepted was due to my low self-esteem and confidence after the accident, the result of my heavy scarring and physical injuries. This need to fit in superseded my usual mindset. I found it to be a cost to my authenticity, which, in hindsight, is a very high price to pay. When I think about it now, I was being someone else I thought I needed to be, and it was also because of my low self-esteem that I didn't like myself very much at all. This was definitely a low period in my life, but it was also a period of great learning.

I learned that the main person to get me out of this mindset was myself. It took a lot of self-talk, self-reflection, and learning not to care what other people thought of my scarring and injuries. For a period, I was unable to wear T-shirts and sleeveless tops because I wanted to conceal the skin graft on my right arm. I also preferred wearing stockings, knee-length or longer skirts, and pants that covered the scars on my thighs. It took a lot of nerve for me even to show the burn garment I was wearing on my right arm, let alone show my arm without it. Each summer, I would need to dig a little deeper, finding the strength to wear a T-shirt and a pair of shorts that didn't fully cover my thighs. I slowly got used to the stares and preferred when people asked what had happened rather than just stare and not say anything. Most people thought I had been badly burned due to the skin grafts and would ask if this was the case. Eventually, it was less of an issue, and I can now wear T-shirts, sleeveless shirts, and shorts without worrying about what I look like or what other people think.

I understand my injuries and scarring are slight compared to those of others; however, I now understand how people feel when they are disfigured or badly scarred by an accident. The person is the same on the inside; appearance doesn't count for much if you don't focus on it. I learned that most people don't tend to notice your scarring and injuries when you don't let it become the centre of attention. I learned that whatever you give your energy to will become a main focus, so if you do not want it to be your main focus, then don't give it your energy. You may think this is trivial, but when you have experienced scarring and disfigurement and must learn to live with it, and when the biggest thing you had to deal with previously was acne, it definitely becomes a big thing. They were big things for me to deal with psychologically, emotionally, and physically. For me, there was a certain amount of anxiety attached to wearing short sleeves which initially revealed my burn garment, then my scarred arm once the garment was no longer required. It is something I have become accustomed to, and I no longer have anxiety about my scars. I have learned that my scars are beautiful. They tell their own story, and I often refer to them as my "battle scars"—a reminder of what I have survived.

I have also learned that with age, when you are trying to be someone you are not, you attract the wrong people in your life. I found that when I am authentic, the right people show up. It also doesn't matter how many people like you, because as you age, you realise your circle of friends grows smaller but the quality increases. There is a saying I read that resonates with me: "If everyone likes you, you are doing something wrong." Many years after my accident, upon reflection, I learned I was getting approval from others even at the expense of my own needs (or those of others). I am not proud of this time in my life, but it is one that I accept as part of me and part of what made me who I am today. I'm human and perfectly imperfect, which I have found is exactly the way to be. Now when I think of my closest friends, I can count them on one hand. They are the people who have shown up for me no matter what I have been through and what they have also been through with me. For this, I am forever grateful.

I also learned that there are people who masquerade as friends and that real friends don't kick you when you are down. This was one of the difficult lessons I learned after the passing of my grandmother. It started with not getting enough sleep for a period of about five weeks, sleeping only four or five hours a night. One Saturday morning, during this period of sleeplessness, I suffered the worst anxiety I have ever experienced. When the attack occurred, I could not eat or drink. I could not stop myself from physically trembling. I remember having to keep my arms folded across my midriff to hide the trembling, and every noise was too loud—laughter was an assault on my senses, and I felt numb. My limbs felt heavy, I felt empty, and my face was blank.

This anxiety attack occurred on a day I had to attend a social event I had agreed to before my grandmother's passing, but she had since passed. I almost could not get dressed, and it took all my strength. It then took all my willpower to get myself out the door, into the car, and then out of the car when we arrived at the destination. That's when things got worse. I drew strength from anyone and anywhere I could and could hardly speak. I was a literal mess, and yet, someone who was supposed to be a close friend did not even notice. I am very grateful to the person who did notice, someone who did not know me very well but picked up on my energy as soon as she saw me. She advised me later, at a catch-up when she saw me that day, she said my face had been blank and she knew something was not right, but she wanted to leave me alone and give me my space.

This anxiety attack was the worst I have ever had in my life, and it was a warning sign that something was very, very wrong. I didn't know what was happening to me at the time, and I knew I needed to see my doctor to discuss what had happened. One thing I did know was I knew I never wanted to feel that way again. When I saw my family doctor a couple of days later, I was diagnosed with depression and prescribed antidepressants for three months. I think I was in denial and didn't feel I needed to take them. I remember wanting to stop taking them after the first monthly check-in with my doctor, but in hindsight, I can see they really did help. This is my experience. I am not advocating the use of medication to treat depression, but it worked for me at my worst as a short-term solution.

Anyone who has experienced anxiety or depression may have a different experience. As I have said, there is no right or wrong, only different. My doctor prescribed half the dose due to my slighter frame and Asian descent, as he felt I couldn't tolerate a full dose, yet I remember feeling the side effects. This was the catalyst in detoxing negative energy from my life. It started with someone who masqueraded as a close friend and kicked me while I was in the depths of my depression. I no longer count that person as a friend or consider they were ever a true friend. I had felt a sense of disconnect with this person previously, and I had been slowly pulling away from the friendship, especially in the last two and a half years prior to my grandmother's passing. There were observances that did not sit well with me and things that she said and did (or didn't say or do) that spoke volumes, confirming the energy I was receiving. Being kicked while I was down was the catalyst to remove such toxic people and energy from my life.

I have provided the following advice to my daughter: True friends do not kick you when you are down. They support and encourage you and want you to feel okay. The person I count as my closest friend is like a brother to me, and upon hearing what had happened, he said to me, "You don't need people like that in your life." I have to agree; the person who kicked me when I was down was one of the people I detoxed from my life, and my life has been better for it. It was a difficult lesson, but I now realise I had to have. I did feel sad that I had lost what I thought was a good, long-lasting friendship, built up over a decade, but upon reflection, I see now it was never a real friendship.

Friendships are about give-and-take on both sides, and I felt the giving was predominantly coming from my side. Detoxing a lot of negative energy in my life, especially in the last year, in the wake of my grandmother's passing, has been a journey in itself. It has been a difficult period of adjustment for me, but it has also been a period of great learning. I have to admit, it was painful, but there were lessons I needed to learn and learning to be comfortable with the uncomfortable was a great learning journey for me—and still is. The lessons I learned and that I am still learning resulted in growth and will continue long after I have written these words. I learned to surround myself with people who support, encourage, and rejoice in my successes—big or small. I am also able to provide them with the same support, encouragement, and joy for their successes. The saying "Your tribe becomes your vibe" is very accurate; the people and energy you surround yourself with become a reflection of the person you are. If you don't like who you are becoming, examine the people you spend the most time with and their effect on you. The thoughts, words, people, habits, and actions you surround yourself with also become yours over time. I learned I needed to make sure they were ones that aligned with who I really am instead of what other people wanted or expected of me.

In regards to friendship, I often advise my daughter, who is now a teenager, that friendships change. There are friends who come into your life for a reason, a season, or a lifetime. If you are fortunate, you may have some friends who may fit all these categories. Some may fit only one or two, and a few are friends for a lifetime. I've been lucky to have a close friend for a lifetime. We have known each other since kindergarten, and the friendship now spans over forty years! We've had our ups and downs—I tend to mention him as a good friend but often say he's like a brother because we have known each other for most of our lives. This is also the friend who advised my husband to take his wife to Europe! It's a friendship that has endured. We don't live in each other's pockets, but even if we haven't seen each other in a while, it's as if no time has passed; we just pick up where we left off and catch up on everything that has happened in our lives. I'm grateful to have him as a lifetime friend.

My other close friendships have all spanned over ten years, up to over twenty years. It is nice to realise people who you have known for a long time have always been there for you, even if you didn't realise it at the time. Or they tend to show up and be more present in your life during difficult times. For these friends, I am very grateful. They restore my faith in people, and it's nice to be reminded I have people to turn to in times of need.

Due to my depression, I have identified my triggers and have been removing or decreasing the impact of these triggers. I found the following main triggers for me:

- Sleep—lack of
- Negative energy/ people
- Food—healthy choices
- Exercise—life's natural antidepressant

The biggest trigger for me is sleep—or specifically lack thereof. The biggest contributor to my anxiety and depression was lack of sleep for a period of four to five weeks before my diagnosis. Due to my experience, ensuring I get adequate sleep (especially when I feel more tired than usual) is most important, including make-up sleep when I can get it. Not getting enough sleep can make you unwell and bring about many complications.

Another trigger is negative energy or people. As a result, I have removed, unfriended, and unfollowed people on social media if I feel they no longer inspire or motivate me in positive ways. I have also removed people who use social media as a surveillance camera to observe my life, using it as a source of gossip. I haven't felt any loss or regret doing this; it actually feels quite liberating, as though a weight has been lifted from my shoulders. Only one person has requested to be re-added since I have done this, and I feel this proves who is interested in keeping in touch rather than using me as a source of gossip, something in which I don't like to participate in. When I found someone's energy was affecting me this way, I did not like who I was becoming, so would distance myself from their energy (except following my accident, when I didn't like myself—a period I am not proud of). I've learned life is too short to spend it with people who do not genuinely care about you.

Another trigger I have worked on is food—specifically, types of food. I have been conscious of how food affects me, remediating any intolerances I may have been ignoring. I've found what foods work for me and how they work for me. This strategy helps my overall health and wellbeing.

Another important trigger is exercise, again the lack thereof. I now find time to exercise regularly, even if it is as simple as taking our dog for a walk. Exercise has been proven to be a natural antidepressant, and I have noticed that when I do not exercise (or do not exercise enough), my mental health deteriorates. I used to exercise daily in my twenties; however, after having my daughter, I've found ways to exercise that fit in with my life and can be done without having to go to the gym. Previously, in my late teens to late twenties, I used to go to the gym every day. Then, in my thirties, it became a few days a week. I felt I wasn't exercising if I didn't go to the gym. Once I reached my forties, I realised I could exercise when and where I liked, and I discovered I preferred exercising outdoors rather than inside a gym. I now regularly practise yoga, strength training, walking, and running 5 km every week. I have found that including exercise in my life in a way that suits me lets me continue the practice. I have also learned to be less harsh on myself if I do not exercise. Sometimes your body just needs rest. Changing my mindset and habits has contributed to better mental health and physical benefits. I have shared a TED Talk in the references section given by neuroscientist Wendy Suzuki, who talks about the brain-changing benefits of exercise. In this talk, Wendy explains the change and transformative effects exercise can have on your brain.

As mentioned previously, during the last six to seven years, I have felt a greater surge in my spiritual (rather than religious) awareness. I have always questioned my religion and did not agree with everything I was taught. I was brought up as a Roman Catholic, and although it has its good points, there are also many with which I disagree. I am not going to get into a conversation about religion here, as everyone has their opinion, and I respect them all. For me, it is more about transformation into a spiritual awakening, one that makes me realise the connection of all humans, all living things, and the earth. We are all connected.

For me, spirituality does not mean I don't believe in a higher being. I do believe there is a divine higher being and that there is a force greater than us. I also believe in guardian angels and that my grandma is one of mine, watching over me. For me, spirituality is practising and growing in compassion, love, empathy, and understanding. For me, it is being more self-aware and grateful. I also believe we manifest things in our lives with our thoughts, behaviours, and actions. Radiating grateful vibes is very powerful! When you are grateful for what you have, you find more to be grateful for in abundance, and gratefulness often attracts more still to be grateful for! Often, I have found the things I am grateful for are not *things* at all, which makes them all the more cherished—for example, the ability of sight, a physically able body, good health, the ability to learn and be curious.

What are you grateful for? Can you list at least three things right now? It helps to ponder on this; consider making it a daily practice to see how it changes your outlook. This is something I practice with my daughter. I regularly ask her what she is grateful or thankful for each day, and I also share what I am grateful for.

During this journey, one of change and transformation, learning about and dealing with anxiety and depression have led me to learning how to transform thoughts and perceptions. This learning has not been just for myself but also for my daughter, helping with her anxiety. Her anxiety was triggered by bullying in the last two and a half years of primary school. I didn't understand what was happening at the time and didn't realise her physical symptoms were a result of anxiety. She had many tummy upsets and vomiting, which became all the more upsetting for her because she felt she had no one to talk to about what was happening. Much of the bullying was covert. When she felt she could finally tell her dad and me what was happening, it was both a relief and a kick in the stomach for me. I could not believe my child was going through something I would not wish on anyone and she felt she had no one to turn to. Finally getting to the root cause, we were able to help her learn different strategies through visits with a child psychologist. The biggest lesson learned during this process is the critical importance of loving and listening to your child, making sure they know their feelings are valid and that they can express how they are feeling to you, their parent. I am very grateful we are able to help my daughter, and she is doing much better now. She has since started high school, made some great friends, and is enjoying school again. Managing her anxiety has become a lot easier, and we have become proactive to ensure we nip it in the bud to prevent it from overwhelming my daughter again.

One of the strategies we found that helps immensely, and which we still practice to this day, is meditation. My daughter and I have gained so much from this practice to calm our minds and transform how we choose to respond rather than react. I find this is a continual learning process, and learning to respond is something that takes practice. To me, it is about being aware of your emotions and what is happening, then learning to choose a response rather than letting your pre-learned habits and emotions react to what is happening around or to you. A simple application for this is catching public transport to and from work. I used to work once a week at a location where I had to change trains and wait for a different line, then walk about fifteen minutes to the office. Then I'd do the reverse for the trip going home, and it would extend my travel time by half an hour, so total travel time was more than one and a half hours, door to door—a total of three hours or more. A few times, when waiting for a train on the different line, the train I needed to catch would either be cancelled or be delayed by about half an hour. This is when I realised I had a choice: I could let myself react, allow my emotions to take over, be annoyed or angry and let it ruin my day, or choose to accept what happened as it was outside my control and find a way to manage it. I chose to accept and manage. It happened on numerous occasions on this train line. I chose to email or call the office to let them know there was a delay, advising them I was on my way and would be arriving late. The walk was also long, but most of it was through parklands, so I also chose to enjoy being surrounded by parklands, wetlands, trees, flowers, birds, and people walking their dogs along the way. I've found the best way to apply this is to ask, "How could I apply this strategy and choose to respond rather than react in everyday life?" Learning how to respond takes practice, but when implemented daily or in small actions, it becomes easier to make a part of your mental strategy.

Meditation has also helped to become more mindful, to be present in life. I have learned to keep my attention on what is happening in the moment rather than be distracted by other things. Showing gratitude also helps change our mindset, being grateful for what we have rather than what we don't have. Another example of where we focus our energy is realising the abundance we already have, which manifests positive, abundant energy. The book *The Plastic Mind*, by Sharon Begley, discusses the effects of meditation. The book discusses the plasticity of the brain and how it continues in adulthood, as it was previously thought that neuroplasticity ceased once you became an adult. It also discusses the science behind how meditation changes your brain.

Research has been conducted with Buddhist monks to see how it affects their brain, confirming meditation changes the brain. They performed scans during meditation to see how it changed their brain. The Mind and Life Institute was founded by His Holiness the Dalai Lama, along with neuroscientists, scientists, and the like. The Dalai Lama has been interested in investigating the brain function of monks who have practised for many years to investigate how their brain function might have been changed by their practice (Hamilton 2015). The book discusses the Dalai Lama's support and encouragement for research on meditation. There is a scientist who was part of the research findings who became a monk and now practices meditation daily. His name is Matthieu Ricard. He has given a few fascinating TED Talks, which I encourage you to listen to. One I have watched a couple of times is titled "How to let altruism be your guide," which he gave in 2015. I have also provided a link to this TED Talk in the references section so you can view it. I have found that practising daily meditation results in a calmer, more thoughtful response to situations and people. It has also helped me to become aware of and recognise my emotions so I can choose how to respond. This is something I will continue to practise as I can see the benefits –, the change in my thought processes and mindset. It's one of the tools I have found to be fundamental to mental wellness.

Overall, the strategies that have worked for me are meditation, regular sleep, and exercise, along with a balanced diet. As you can see, these are well-proven strategies that work for various people of all walks of life, cultures, beliefs, and genders. They are also not radical and can be practised by anyone. However, for most people, they tend to be difficult to maintain. I find if you practise and implement them in small steps, it becomes easier to increase or add to the actions incrementally. By ensuring I get enough sleep, eat well, and exercise regularly, as well as keeping a healthy mind through meditation, I am able to manage my depression and anxiety.

I have found that choosing your mindset and being open to other perspectives helps to expand your experience. Balance is important, and yet balance is different for everyone. There have been times when balance may be affected, for example, by major exams or assessments or unforeseen circumstances, such as illness or unexpected events, but once they pass, I will re-balance what is out of balance. This ensures I maintain a healthy mind, body, and spirit. I have learned that you can always come up with excuses not to exercise or eat well; however, the only person you are cheating is yourself. If you start small, then increase the momentum, it becomes easier to keep those actions in place. Also, when you do stop these actions, you feel the adverse impact quite rapidly, and it is your responsibility to take action to reverse the impact. Taking accountability for your life, thoughts, behaviours, and actions is challenging, but as a coach, I have found that accountability is the biggest contributor to my coachees' success. When you realise you get out what you put in and that only you can get you where you need or want to be, you will make an effort to take those small steps to bring you closer to your goals. This applies to all areas of your life. If you feel accountability is your weakness, it may help to have an accountability partner. This may be a coach, mentor, partner, friend, or colleague—find what works for you.

Upon reading about my experiences here and learning about my journey, some might think this journey is not one of change and transformation but rather of finding myself again. This is partly true, because there are practices and interests I did not pursue for fear of not fitting in or being accepted, which I now embrace. I felt the courage to let go of the fear of being judged and embraced my interests and practices, even those that were unconventional. However, I feel that finding myself is part of my transformation, transforming into the person I am meant to be, not the person I was expected to become. Learning to challenge my beliefs and assumptions and change some of them has been overwhelming at times, yet it has helped me to grow as a person. Even the painful experiences are lessons, and I often look for the lesson to be learned from a situation rather than wonder why it is happening. Everything happens for a reason. Sometimes it takes a little longer to find out what the reason is, maybe because we need to accept what we already know or don't like to move on. I have learned that it is often in my discomfort when there has been the most growth, whether that be in life, family, work, or study. I have also found my acceptance of what I cannot change and that growth takes time and cannot be rushed—no matter how uncomfortable it may be!

Over the following pages, I have summarised a list of learnings and their applications, based on experiences and observances of my grandmother and mother and my own life's challenges. I hope they challenge, motivate, and inspire you to pursue your own learning journey—enjoying both the positive benefits and growth relating to the adverse aspects of your journey.

Learnings

These learnings are based on observations and personal experience. I feel my grandma lived the first two, which helped her face life's challenges:

Celebrate wins, especially the small wins.

We often forget to celebrate the small wins. This is something I remind my coachees to practice. Often, when I ask my coachees to list their wins for the first time, they are not sure what to say. Once I ask them some more questions about things they may have been working on or accomplished in the past week, day, or month, they realise they do have wins they can acknowledge and celebrate. These small wins often lead us to the bigger wins or goals we are working towards. They help keep us focussed and motivated to continue moving forward. The pace doesn't matter as long as you are continuously moving forward towards your goals. Moving forward is important. As long as there is movement in the right direction, no matter how small, you are making progress. Celebrating the small wins remind you what you are working towards and keeps you focussed on achieving the bigger picture. When you recognise each small action or step achieved, you are motivated to continue on the journey to obtain your larger goal.

A personal application of this is celebrating each small win on my learning journey as I complete my MBA. I focus on each task, assessment, and exam for each individual subject. As I complete each one, I celebrate it in a way that is befitting and then focus on the next task or action required. As I complete an assessment, I celebrate each time I receive a passing grade. By doing this, I have successfully completed my first year with a GPA of 5.50! This has motivated me to continue, realising I am able to juggle family, work, and study successfully. I let go of the fear that I would not be able study after a long period (more than twenty years) by focussing on each step. This brings me closer to the end goal—graduating with my master of business administration. I have completed the first year successfully, leaving only two more to complete! When I enrolled a year ago, my anxiety and doubts surfaced, and I wondered if I was finally ready to pursue it, but as I worked through each subject and passed, I realised the effort required to complete each subject and became more familiar with the style of writing required. I also became better at prioritising and dedicating the time required to complete the research and write the required reports for each assessment. Each step I added to my learning journey resulted in another win to celebrate.

Have an attitude of gratitude.

Choosing to have an attitude of gratitude is very powerful. When we are grateful for what or who we have in our lives, there seems to be more to be grateful for. The vibes you give out are often the vibes that come back to you. This mindset takes practice, but you can start small. For example, think of something you are grateful or thankful for each day and then increase the number or write what you are grateful for in a gratitude journal. You could also use them as affirmations each day.

As mentioned, I like to ask my daughter to think about what she is grateful for each day, often at the end of the day, before she goes to sleep. However, occasionally, I will ask at different times of the day, because sometimes our conversation brings us to the topic of gratitude. Often, small and simple things come to mind. I then like to share with my daughter what I am grateful for as well. This is something small we can share together and keep practising our mindset to focus our energy on what we are grateful and thankful for rather than bemoaning our hardships. I have found this to be a continuously evolving mindset that I have practised daily, especially in the last twelve months. Applying gratitude is where I have observed the biggest effects and learning on this journey.

The next learning is to surround yourself with those who truly love you, support you, and are there for you when you need them.

Remember those who love you. Don't worry about people who don't care about you.

Often, we worry too much about what other people think. I have learned that what other people think about me is none of my business. I teach my daughter the same thing. It's important to acknowledge other people's thoughts but not use them to measure your self-worth, especially if they are negative. Remember, you are important, and your life is as meaningful and valid as the next person's. We all contribute to this life in our own way, and however we do is okay as long as we are not harming any living beings, the earth, or ourselves. It is also important to acknowledge that not everyone will share the same views on everything, but this does not mean you cannot learn something from them or that you cannot get along. You may have to agree to disagree on some things, but you can remain friends and be amicable to each other. I remind my daughter that not everyone thinks the same as we do, and we should celebrate our differences. "How boring would it be if we all liked the same thing, did the same thing, and all looked the same?" I have often asked her.

Think about our various tastes in food, clothes, and music. I find this applies to people as well: there are those who are soft like a melody or ballad, then there are those who are hard and harsh like heavy grunge metal. Then there are all those people in between, many variations. However, it is important to remember those people who are like melodies or grunge metal, although different to us, may compliment and encourage our own song. We may be drawn to people out of habit; however, when you take the time to reflect on who loves you, it benefits to focus on that energy and keep those people around you There are plenty of people who are great pretenders, they will say and do the right things in front of others yet their intentions are not. I have found it important to test friendships to ensure you have the right people around you, the same applies to family and loved ones. Sometimes family members may love you but not care that much about your wellbeing and success. I have found it is important to observe the energy around you and know the difference.

It is important to trust your intuition. Research has shown that your gut is like your second brain and that gut instincts are an important indicator to heed. Think about the times you did not pay attention to your gut instincts. How was your overall experience? Also, pay attention to people who show you they care with their actions, not just words. Their actions should fill you with positive feelings, leaving you feeling supported and cared for, not feeling as though you are unimportant to them and provide them no benefit.

Be joyful.

There may be times when you don't or can't feel joy but you can always choose to be joyful or find the joy in adverse circumstances. Sometimes it might mean looking a little harder. Even though my grandmother and mother experienced hardship and heartbreak, they remained joyful. It is often difficult to do when your experience is not joyful. Pretending to be joyful can take a lot of energy, as I found when I was diagnosed with depression. However, this helped me to appreciate all emotions and to truly appreciate joy. We often need to experience the negative emotions to appreciate the positive ones. I have also learned that joyfulness comes in many forms and can be expressed in just as many forms. There can be quick, small moments of joy along with greater, more significant moments, yet they are all important. Small moments might include a ray of sunshine through the clouds, a smile of appreciation, a hug, or a cool breeze on a warm day. Some significant joyful moments could be the first time you drive a car, gaining a sense of independence and freedom, the birth of a child, hearing good news after a prolonged illness, and more. Whatever the reason, being joyful lifts your spirit as well as those of others and reminds us to enjoy these moments, as they can be fleeting.

You never stop learning.

This is the greatest lesson I learned from my mom. Whether it's from academic sources or thorough life experiences, learning is a lifelong journey. My mother did not finish her high school education, and as a result, she values opportunities for formal learning and encourages her children and grandchildren to embrace the opportunity to learn. My mum also realises that you can learn from anyone at any age, whether it is from her grandchildren, children, or people older than her. This is because younger generations may be learning about things we were not exposed to when we were in school, and things have changed since my school days. It's also the realisation that learning is also not limited to formal education—knowledge and information can be learned from many sources throughout life.

Learning can challenge you and enable you to grow. My growth from my own learnings, especially in the last twelve months, has been challenging and surprising yet also very welcome. My self-reflection has challenged me, enabled growth, and enabled me to let go of long-standing fears. The formal learning associated with studies challenges me and keeps me moving forward towards graduating with an MBA, something I have wanted to do for a few years but never felt brave enough or ready to explore. However, this changed last year, when I received a message from a learning institution advising I might be eligible to complete an MBA. I opened it to read and submitted an application. I soon received a phone call, submitting further documentation before receiving a letter of offer for a place to study in their program. This seemed to happen seamlessly, in a matter of a few days. So far, the first year of study has been a challenging yet rewarding journey. I have two more years to complete before graduating. I'm excited and motivated to continue the learning process. It has been challenging to juggle life, family, work, and study, but I have found that if you truly want something, you will make it happen. Learning something new is not limited to age, only by your own perception of the learning process. As I have said, learning is a lifelong journey, a sentiment shared by the institution where I am completing my MBA.

Self-reliance and accountability—be responsible for your own life, happiness, and health.

Among the major strengths my grandmother and mother possessed are self-reliance and accountability. Throughout their lives, they learned to be resourceful, and they became self-reliant. This does not mean they never asked for or received help from others, but they did not rely on such help. They learned that the main person to rely on was themselves, and they were in charge of their life and mindset. That taking accountability for your thoughts, behaviours, and feelings is important to manifest what you want in your life.

By not placing blamee on other people or events, we recognise there are adverse consequences for our choices, thoughts, and actions. My close friend said to me that he dislikes hearing people complain about things but are unwilling to change. Why waste your energy complaining about things in your life if you are not willing to take any action to better the situation? My grandmother and mother did not complain about where life took them or what circumstances they found themselves in. They got on with living their lives and did what they needed to do, to care for their families and—to a lesser extent—themselves. It's not that they didn't have their moments; they are human after all and are entitled to feel anger, frustration, grief, and loss. However, it is what you do with those emotions that matters. I have found when we own our emotions, our actions, and our behaviours, we can accept them for what they are and then let them go. For example, when we are angry at someone and hold onto that anger, does it benefit you or the other person? The Buddha said, "Holding onto anger is like drinking poison and expecting the other person to die."

Let that sink in for a moment.

When I read this quote, I realised that learning to forgive and let go of your anger results in your own inner peace. This does not mean you should forget how others have treated you, but you should learn to let it go so you can move on. Move forward, and don't let it eat you up inside. Again, this is a practice that is difficult to learn and put into action. However, once you have mastered it, energy will flow effortlessly through your life.

Enjoy nice things, moments, and people, but do not become attached to them.

My grandmother and mother both have elegant taste. They have been able to enjoy luxury in their lives, and are grateful for the experience. However, they do not become attached to material possessions, are not easily impressed by them, and do not feel they increase their self-worth. My mother grew up surrounded by many expensive brands due to her uncle's business, bringing in imported goods from Europe and the United States. My mother wore some amazing clothes and accessories. She is tall for a Vietnamese woman (168 cm) and is attractive, so her uncle liked her to model his wares. As a result, people would ask where her clothes and accessories came from or what products she used, so it was essentially free marketing for my uncle. My mother appreciated this and came to realise what good quality looked and felt like. My mother also came to realise that good things do not always last. One of her favourite expressions is "Easy come, easy go."

The lesson here is if you haven't earned your goods and your trust in people/places, they do not tend to last. There is no longevity in things provided to you that you have not worked hard for. When people win the lottery, for example, the extraordinary amount of money they win tends not to last. They also learn who cares about them, rather than just their money. There is truth in the saying "Death and money brings out the best *and* the worst in people." I have read articles where people who have won large sums of money were revisited some years after their win and were not better off, as they had spent it all on frivolous things or people. I have found this applies to anything I have worked hard for. This has taught me that while I can enjoy nice things, moments, and people, I must not attach great importance or worth to them. They may form part of cherished memories, and I feel these are to be enjoyed; however, I have found that attaching yourself to them can have a detrimental effect on your life. Attachment makes us feel as though we cannot live or do anything without these things, people, or moments. We become accustomed to the highs or lows they provide and pursue that feeling without realising the consequences of these actions. Take the following examples:

- *Wealth.* A person who appears to have everything they could ever want in regards to money, material possessions, travel, and experiences yet does not feel fulfilled, happy, or satisfied with what they have.
- *Social media.* We feel a sense of elation when we receive many likes or follows following a post, but this results in a need for more likes, and more frequent posting, to increase the frequency of likes and follows.

Attachment to the elation these things provide, can elicit adverse consequences if not managed well, such as anxiety and depression. Therefore, it's an important learning not to associate our happiness or worth with things, moments, and people.

Regularly detox negative energy.

Following my depression diagnosis, my doctor expressed it was important for me to concentrate on getting better. It was important for me to detox from anyone or anything affecting me negatively in the long term. I learned to notice how people and their energy affected me. I also noticed the type of energy present in my home and surroundings and how to manage it. I researched smudging with sage leaves, which helps to clear bad energy from your space. Based on one article I read, smudging is believed to have origins in the Native American tribes. This ancient ritual involves burning sage leaves with the aim of cleansing energy—good and bad—in the space surrounding us. We can liken this to a "spiritual spring clean" for our homes. When you think about how we regularly clean our homes from physical dust and dirt, it also makes sense to cleanse it from energies that may be present (Lee 2018). When I learned about the ritual of smudging, I performed it in the house we were renting to cleanse out as much negative energy as I could. I then burnt sage incense in the evenings when our family ate dinner together to cleanse any unwanted energies each day. When we bought our new home, after I picked up the keys and before we moved in, I performed a smudging ritual, and I still burn sage incense daily during dinner to cleanse any unwanted energies.

We have also become more mindful of who we invite to our home, as well as who stays over, to protect our sacred space. The energy in our home is very different now, and people who have visited comment on how the energy is peaceful in our new home. Detoxing negative people from your life may prove difficult; however, when you realise how the energy of these people affects you, it becomes easier to do. As I have mentioned, the people you surround yourself with are crucial; your tribe becomes your vibe. This relates to friends, colleagues, and even family members. I understand you cannot remove a toxic family member from your life completely, but you can limit your exposure to their toxic energy. Think of how you want to be treated and how you want your immediate family to be treated. Your work environment is also important, because you spend so much of your waking hours with your colleagues. Having boundaries helps to manage negative people and energy. These boundaries are not for other people; they are for *you*.

Self-love and self-care are paramount.

We have all heard this many times. I never used to think it was that important—until my grandmother passed away. After my depression diagnosis, sitting in my doctor's office, he advised me to take time for myself. He also advised me it was not selfish to ensure I looked after my mental and physical health. Previously, I would have shrugged it off, but this time, I decided I would take a week for myself. I called my manager and sent through the doctor's certificate confirming my diagnosis. I had a week of leave. I took myself offline—no social media and no digital devices. I decided to do things I had been putting off because I had no one to accompany me. I decided I would go, do, and see— just for me. This was something I had never done before. There have been times I was afraid to be on my own, worrying what other people might think of me being by myself. Now, when I think about it, I was just holding myself back from enjoying these things. Now, I did not care. My main focus was to rest, look after myself, and do what I needed to do in my week, without anyone knowing what I was doing. It was so liberating! I did things I wanted to do and stopped paying attention to things that did not matter. That week, I looked after my little family, and during the hours my daughter was at school, I indulged in what I had been putting off and simply enjoyed. These activities nurtured my soul. I visited the art gallery to view an exhibition I had put off seeing, and I went to see a movie.

I finally went to see *Sculptures by the Sea*, an art exhibition along the coast of Bondi to Tamarama (NSW, Australia). Every year, I would say I wanted to see the exhibition, and each year would pass without me going to see it. I finally went to see it in 2018. The weather was beautiful—a warm sunny day with a nice breeze. It was the right weather to be walking along the coast, viewing the wonderful art works on display. It was definitely food for my soul.

During this week of self-love and self-care, I didn't take or make any phone calls or messages until I felt ready. I disconnected until I was ready to reconnect again. I did things on my terms, and it was wonderful. It was a week where I nurtured myself—my mind, body, and spirit! I even took myself out for a nice lunch. I found when I was comfortable and enjoyed my own company, it was more meaningful when I did have company, because it was a choice, not an obligation. I learned during that week how important self-love and self-care really are. I learned to embrace my faults and shortcomings and accept them as part of who I am. I accepted all of me, even the anxious and depressed parts of myself. I learned to love all of me—the good, the not so good, and the bad, and I learned that it was okay.

When you love yourself and nurture yourself, you are better able to look after others. We mothers tend to overlook our needs, tending to our family's needs. When we do this repeatedly, we become empty; we burn out and we become exhausted. If we don't look after ourselves, then we can't expect anyone else to do it for us. We've all heard, "If you don't look after yourself, no one else will." I learned how true that phrase is. When we love ourselves, accepting everything we like and dislike, we then can love others in the same way. It is important to find a way to love yourself, warts and all. Remember, we are human. We are not meant to be perfect. Our flaws and imperfections are what makes us who we are.

All this leads me to the final learning which for me has become the most important on my journey:

Become someone who you would like if you met you or someone you needed when you were younger.

Think about who you are as a person. If you met you, would you like who you are? I had a conversation with a friend who was concerned about her daughter's behaviour since starting high school. I asked who her daughter surrounded herself with and whether they were the kind of people she would benefit having around her. My friend also advised she was disappointed about a specific situation and how her daughter had responded. I asked my friend because she has informed me she wasn't always a "good" child growing up (but then who was?), "Who did you need when you were growing up?"

She answered, "Someone who was supportive and could help me."

I asked, "Could you be that person for your daughter?"

She paused to ponder that.

As parents, we often forget we were once in our children's shoes, maybe anxious or rebellious teenagers—or both! I have also felt the same as my friend at times and have found it helps to pause and think about it from a different perspective. It also helps to be who you are meant to be before society, family, and cultural expectations told you who you should be. We grow up with societal norms, family, and cultural expectations, as well as our own harsh self-criticism. I have found if you love yourself, accepting your faults as well as your strengths, you can be someone you would like you meet. This may be the very person the younger you needed in their life. Again, I have found this is not an easy feat. Because we are human, we are imperfect. What helps make this easier is practice. As I have mentioned, I don't believe practice makes perfect. Practice makes permanent. The more we practice, the more these practices become permanent, a part of who we are. So, with practice, we can love and embrace who we are becoming. Who are you becoming?

Précis

* *

*Y*ou usually know what you need to do. However, due to fear, you may be unable to let go of what prevents you from progressing. I hope as you read my learnings, something resonated with you and sparked curiosity to embark on your own learning journey. Remember to get out of your own way and allow yourself to be free—of fear and of judgement. Learn to embrace changes as they occur instead of resisting change. Yes, the journey may be uncomfortable at times, but when you think about it, does any journey ever guarantee comfort?

I have learned to find what works for you in regard to your health—mental, physical, and spiritual. Listen to your intuition and let love guide you in your decisions. I have learned to trust myself, practise self-reflection, and let go of anything or anyone that may be holding me back—even when it is me! Thank you for joining me on my learning journey to face everything and rise. Writing this book has been a great form of creative expression, and as Albert Einstein said, "Creativity is intelligence having fun." This was also a lot of fun. Peace and blessings!

It takes a lot of courage to release the familiar and seemingly secure, to embrace the new. But there is no real security in what is no longer meaningful. There is more security in the adventurous and exciting, for in movement there is life, and in change there is power.

—Alan Cohen

Symbolism during My Journey

* *

*T*here have been specific images I have been drawn to during my journey, and I would like to share these findings with you. They are by no means the only resources available, and I encourage you to do your own research since we have information readily available, literally at our fingertips.

The imagery on the cover of this book has special significance. When my grandma was unwell and near her death, whenever I went for a walk, dragonflies would fly across my path. I noticed this on two or three occasions, not realising my grandmother was quite unwell and about to pass. It was in hindsight that I learned the significance of the dragonfly. What prompted me to look up the meaning of dragonflies was when I received a bereavement card from a friend, featuring beautiful dragonflies. I remembered seeing dragonflies in the weeks leading up to my grandmother's passing, so I thought there must be a significance. Also, on more than one occasion after my grandmother's death, there would be a red dragonfly hovering for a few seconds before flying away. I looked up the meaning of dragonflies, which resonated with my experience, and I came to realise their significance. I found this regarding the symbolism of the dragonfly:

> The main symbolisms of the dragonfly are renewal, positive force and the power of life in general. Dragonflies can also be a symbol of the sense of self that comes with maturity. Also, as a creature of the wind, the dragonfly frequently represents change.

> And as a dragonfly lives a short life, it knows it
> must live its life to the fullest with the short time it
> has—which is a lesson for all of us. (Langley 2013)

Another mention regarding the symbolism of dragonflies is below:

> In almost every part of the world, the Dragonfly
> symbolizes change, transformation, adaptability,
> and self-realization. (Dragonfly Transitions 2020)

I also found an article in the *Daily Breeze* detailing the significance of a red dragonfly. The article states that the Japanese consider red dragonflies to be "very sacred," offering a symbol of courage, strength, and happiness, especially after hard times (Grenier 2016).

There is also an article in *Dragonfly Times* that details the sightings of the red dragonfly; they often appear to people surrounding life episodes of loss and death (Horkan 2012).

Whether or not you believe in the spiritual significance of dragonflies, I hope they provide interesting reading and provoke thought. If you would like to read more about the meaning of dragonflies, you may wish to read information from the *Power of Positivity* website, which provides further detail. I have provided a link in the references section for you to access and read in your own time.

Again, please feel free to conduct your own research and not be limited by my findings. I was drawn to dragonflies without realising their significance, and I even had one tattooed on the inside of my wrist in memory of my grandmother after her passing. I did this because it provided a permanent reminder of my grandmother. I feel each time I see a dragonfly, I feel it is her spirit visiting me, giving me strength. So, upon discovering their symbolic meaning, it resonated with me, and I realised the synchronicity.

I found I was drawn to the lotus flower, especially pink lotus flowers, which is significant in its own right. I found the following excerpt from a handout by Binghamton University, which helped me understand the significance.

> The Lotus flower is regarded in many different cultures, especially in eastern religions, as a symbol of purity, enlightenment, self-regeneration and rebirth.

The colour of the lotus flower also has significance across different cultures. There is information regarding the meaning of lotus flowers by Ravenscroft, and I have provided links in the references section. Again, please feel free to perform your own research for more information. In Buddhism, the Lotus flower being a symbol of purity, enlightenment, and rebirth - characteristics which are a perfect analogy for the human condition: even when its roots are in the dirtiest and muddiest of waters, the Lotus produces the most beautiful flower (Nan Tien Temple 2020). I interpret this to mean that even if you grow up in less ideal conditions, you can still blossom into a beautiful soul.

Another symbol I was drawn to is the "om" symbol. Again, I did some research, and I read on one website that the "om symbol is very powerful and can hold significance because many people can relate to it. The symbol is one of peace, tranquility and unity and reminds people to slow down and breathe" (One Tribe Apparel 2018). The origins of the om symbol are from ancient Hindu text. These texts are associated with Vedanta, one of the six Hindu philosophies. "They regard the meaning of the Om symbol as inexhaustible, infinite language and knowledge, and the essence everything that exists and of life itself." The om sound is a short "seed" mantra, chanted to connect with and energize the chakras. The om symbol represents the sound in a visual form and holds a lot of meaning. Om is one of the most important spiritual symbols and is found throughout many ancient Hindu texts, prayers, and ceremonies (One Tribe Apparel 2018).

I was drawn to these "symbols" due to my own spiritual growth. As I researched, I learned their history and symbolism, and they became even more interesting and relevant. I hope it was for you as well.

References

Binghampton University, Institute for Asia and Asian Diasporas, Meaning of the Lotus Flower—handout, https://www.binghamton.edu/iaad/outreach/Meaning%20 of%20the%20Lotus%20Flower%20-%20%20handout.pdf

Definition of Synchronicity, https://www.dictionary.com/browse/synchronicity

Dragonfly Transitions, 2020, 'Why the Dragonfly?', https://dragonflytransitions.com/why-the-dragonfly/

Ferris, T, 2017, 'Why you should define your fears instead of your goals', TED Talks, https://www.ted.com/talks/tim_ferriss_why_you_should_define_your_fears_instead_of_your_goals?language=en

Grenier, M, 2016, 'Red dragonfly brings serenity in moments of despair', Dailybreeze https://www.dailybreeze.com/2016/08/28/red-dragonfly-brings-serenity-in-moments-of-despair/amp/

Hamilton, J, 2005, 'The links between the Dalai Lama and Neuroscience', npr.org, https://www.npr.org/templates/story/story.php?storyId=5008565

Horkan, A, 2012, 'Red dragonfly symbolism and the transformation of death, Dragonfly Times, http://anniehorkan.com/red-dragonfly-symbolism-transformation-death/

Langley, S, 2013, 'How to make unique dragonflies for your garden, https://sierranewsonline.com/how-to-make-unique-dragonflies-for-your-garden/

Lee, N, 2018, 'This is how to do a sage cleanse in your home', 10 Daily, https://10daily.com.au/lifestyle/health/a181001cwg/this-is-how-to-do-a-sage-cleanse-in-your-home-20181001?&utm_medium=paid-search&utm_source=10daily&utm_campaign=digital:na&utm_term=google&utm_content=dsa&gclid=CjwKCAiAu9v wBRAEEiwAzvjq-xic3-7wqYWTLWR Hj3kei-w7FeU-7gjZjCRwPux4wVFxIXAi-yKyNxoCQDwQAvD_BwE

One Tribe Apparel, 2018,'What does the om symbol mean?', One Tribe Apparel website, https://www.onetribeapparel.com/blogs/pai/what-does-the-om-symbol-mean

Post, SG, 2005, 'Altruism, Happiness, and Health: It's Good to Be Good', International Journal of Behavioral Medicine 2005, Vol. 12, No. 2, 66–77

Power of Positivity 2000—2015, https://www.powerofpositivity.com/if-you-see-dragonflies-often-this-is-what-it-means/

Ravenscroft, D, 'Pink Lotus flower meaning', lotusflowermeaning. net and 'Learn about the Meanings and Symbolisms Associated with the Beautiful Lotus Flower", https://www.lotusflowermeaning.net/pink.php https://www.lotusflowermeaning.net/

Ricard, M, 2015, 'How to let altruism be your guide', TED Talks, 'https://www.ted.com/talks/matthieu_ricard_how_to_let_altruism_be_your_guide?language=en

Suzuki, W, 2017, 'The brain-changing benefits of exercise', TEDWomen2017, https://www.ted.com/talks/wendy_suzuki_the_brain_changing_benefits_of_exercise?utm_campaign=tedspread&utm_medium=referral&utm_source=tedcomshare

A percentage of profits for this book will be donated to Beyond Blue. Beyond Blue are an organisation who helps improve the lives of individuals, families and communities affected by anxiety, depression and suicide. Beyond Blue provide support for anxiety, depression and suicide prevention. Research states that mental illness is experienced by one in five Australians (20%) aged 16 to 85 (Facts and Figures about Mental Health, Black Dog Institute, 2018). There is still stigma attached to mental illness, so in writing this book, I hope to lessen the stigma to show even if you experience mental illness, it can be managed and there is support available to ensure mental wellness. I have provided a link to their website which details the support they provide:

https://www.beyondblue.org.au/home

About the Author

. . . .

*D*anThy Nguyen is a qualified life coach, as well as a Learning and Organisational Development Consultant with a career spanning more than twenty years. She enjoys the creative writing process and regularly blogs as a mother, wife, and student.

Printed in the United States
by Baker & Taylor Publisher Services